THE

RIGHTING

WARS I -

THE INITIATION

Other books by M. J. Logan

Maurpikios Fiddler:
The True Meaning of Magic
Book I – Faith

Maurpikios Fiddler:
The Magical Amethyst of Spes
Book II- Hope

Maurpikios Fiddler:
The Red Ruby of Edo
Book III- Love

Coming Soon:

Maurpikios Fiddler:
The Secret of Eden
Book IV

The Righting Wars:
The Infiltration
Book II

THE RIGHTING WARS I -

THE INITIATION

By

M.J. LOGAN

Copyright © 2017 by M.J. Logan.

Library of Congress Control Number: 2017934007

The Righting Wars: Book I—The Initiation

ISBN:
Hardcover: 978-0-9979879-1-1
Softcover: 978-0-9979879-2-8

This is a work of fiction. Names, characters, places, and incidents are either the product of the author's imagination, or are used fictitiously, and any resemblance to any actual persons, living or dead, events, or locales is entirely coincidental.

This book was printed in the United States of America.

Release Date: 07/01/2018

To order additional copies of this book, or to request a copy for review, contact:
Unlimited Potential Publishing
www.mjlogan.net

*For Hillary, who stood as a role model for me
and helped me to be strong long before the world knew her
true strength.*

*For Cillerine, who taught me that it is not what I say,
but how I say it, to choose my battles wisely,
and that the pen is my best weapon.*

Forward ∞

The election season of 2016 was very difficult for me. When Election Day finally arrived, I was nervous all day. What would happen if we wake up tomorrow, and he's our new president?

I went to the polls, placed my vote, and walked away knowing what most people failed to acknowledge—he could actually win this thing. For some strange reason, regardless of what the prediction polls told us, I could sense it in the air. As I stood in line, people I had known for years and had grown up with could hardly look me in the eye. I knew their preferred candidate without them having to say a word, and his entire campaign had been stoked with racism, fear, and division.

As I returned to my car, passing by the markedly long line of people waiting to vote, I spotted a high school friend I adored very much. We had grown up during a time where political divisions did not overtly exist. However, in recent years, the climate of our nation had definitely taken a sharp turn.

Her countenance immediately told me she yearned for the same jovial and cordial conversation we often had after not seeing each other for years. However, just as fast as I noticed her reaction, I sensed her pull back. Fortunately, I did not let that stop me. I smiled, hugged her, gave her a heartfelt, "Hello," and rubbed her shoulder, reassuring her that we would all be okay

But honestly, I wasn't sure if we would be okay. Many who were not a part of the minority failed to sense the danger and fear the rest of us did. Why would they? The insults and threats to our humanity were not aimed at them. I also came to realize through this journey that this was not their fault.

I write this novel with caution. I know many people who are of the majority that supported him are well-meaning, generous, and innately good people. I do not wish to paint any group with a single brush. However, I realize now that more dread existed within me than I was willing to admit. I went home election night oblivious to the fact that there was a great deal more fear invading my subconscious than I was aware of or willing to admit. With my family at my side, we followed the election on CNN the entire evening, which ultimately revealed that my choice for leader of my country—the leader of the free world—had been defeated. I was devastated. I made sure I said a prayer for the United States of America and the entire world. When my prayer was done, I knew God had heard me. I snuggled in my covers with a sense of relief.

Surprisingly, I drifted off to sleep easily. When I awoke, however, tears streamed down my face. My subconscious had answered the question I had asked myself the previous morning. Through the night, a vivid dream had formed in my fantasy-driven mind as to what actually had taken place. I awoke to the terrifying truth that he was now my new president.

I dreamed of a new world and a different America. I dreamed of the United Missions of America. I dreamed of a place that was the result of the election of 2016, an antithesis of the country that I had grown to know, love, and be proud of. I now wish to share this dream with you. Welcome to the United Missions of America.

I pledge allegiance to the flag
Of the United Missions of America
And to the dictators I raise my hand

M.J. Logan

One nation under Jenroe Regime
Which is racially superior
And reigns supreme

Welcome to the past, the present, and the future ∞

Welcome to The Righting Wars!

Chapter 1 ∞
Theft—3016 AD

The Palers from the Medical Mission stormed into the home and seized the baby as Jana Sparrow let out a blood-curdling scream.

"Please, don't take her! Please, she's an innocent child! Philmore, please do something!" Jana screamed at her husband, her eyes pleading with his.

The tiny baby girl, named Piper, had just been born. Philmore gasped when he saw her.

Her skin . . . it was dark.

He raked his trembling fingers through his hair. *This is unconscionable. What have we done? How could things go this wrong so quickly?* His eyes darted back and forth from his wife Jana to his eight-year-old daughter, Keelie, unable to console either.

He saw Keelie crouched in the corner with a tight grip on her tattered brown teddy bear. The terror in her eyes tormented him. He wanted desperately to run to her and scoop her up in his arms. She screamed as the men kicked and shoved her mother, who had just given birth, yet he could do nothing as the Medical Militia continued to hold incinerator guns on him.

"Please, don't take her," Jana cried out over and over again.

The Sparrows had been warned this could happen, yet Philmore never thought it would. He caught another glimpse of the baby girl. She had the same striking blue eyes as Keelie and Jana—but her smooth skin was markedly darker than that of her fair-skinned twin brother who wailed uncontrollably in the bassinet across the room.

Dread spread through him as reality set in. He knew what was next.

The Medical Mission swiftly wrapped the baby girl in a blanket and disappeared through the door into the cold, dark night. It had been just two months since the swearing in of President Jeremy Jenroe, and the nightmare had begun. The law was nothing new. It had been in effect for quite some time. The orders were to cleanse the Americans, and like no other Jenroe before him, Jeremy was determined to enforce the cleansing. Philmore knew his baby daughter, Piper, would be labeled a genetic anomaly and ordered, in compliance with administrative law, to be taken away and placed in the home of a Sunz family to be raised by others with the same dark skin as hers.

That evening, he and Jana would learn that their little Piper was delivered to Righting Territory and placed in the arms of her new mother—Maya Pense.

Philmore's family would never be the same. They would recall the events of that night over and over—the relief in the room as the detector read ambiguous on the twin baby boy, the terrifying moments that followed as the twin baby girl entered the world and the detector read "Sunz," and then the moment she was snatched from her mother's arms and taken into the night.

∞∞∞∞∞∞∞∞∞∞

Miles away, in the dark before dawn, Maya rocked her new baby.

The front door clicked shut. Jenroe's officials had disappeared through it as abruptly as they had come. Maya stared at the door. Her heart pounded in her chest, but she had known that this day would come. She vowed in her heart that she would love and care for this little girl as if she were her own. She took a deep breath. Reaching for the old, worn book, she finally glanced down at Piper and exhaled. Immediately, she knew there was something different about her.

"This . . ." Maya Pense whispered as she held her baby and clung to her Bible, ". . . is a very special child. Thank you, God. I know you have big plans for her."

Chapter 2∞
Betrayal or Not? —the Election of 2016

A thousand years earlier...

The world was in complete shock as Nadold P. Murt, along with his entire family, stood on the ostentatiously decorated stage. Confetti and balloons fell around them as an unprecedented number of supporters celebrated his victory. He was now the 45th president of the United States of America and leader of the most powerful nation in the world. Half of the country was on fire with excitement, the other half holding its breath in anticipation of what was to come. Both cable and local news channels were in a frenzy reporting the unexpected defeat of Democratic Candidate Illaria Clemens.

"America, history has been made!" one station reported. "In a highly unexpected outcome, Nadold P. Murt is now the 45th president of the United States of America."

"Nadold P. Murt has defied results of almost every poll

this election season," reported another. "He has defeated Clemens in a sweeping Electoral College win to become our 45th president!"

Network after network, the response was the same. No one, not even Murt or his own campaign, had been completely confident he would pull it off. Regardless of which network the American people, or the world tuned into, the breaking news was the same. Murt had defeated Clemens. He was now the 45th president of the United States of America...with complete control of America's nuclear codes.

∞∞∞∞∞∞∞∞∞

The first two years of Murt's term passed smoothly enough. He carried out several campaign promises and, other than an occasional remnant of political heat, the rhythm of everyday life lulled the nation back into a political slumber.

Then came that day in the private conference room of the presidential resort, Par La Mer. It was eerily quiet with an air of dissonance as the four powerful leaders secretly negotiated the exchange of the final payment for the construction of the wall. Murt had promised the wall and finally delivered it to the American people. It was now time for him to make good on his promises to Russian President Petrov; North Korean leader

Chang, and Iranian President Mahdavi.

With a steady hand and a countenance of pomposity, Murt, in a dramatic show of histrionics, slowly opened his briefcase. Petrov, Chang, and Mahdavi exchanged knowing glances. Murt revealed the priceless information they would receive for their hefty donation to the $45 billion-dollar wall that now surrounded the United States of America.

Murt, visibly pleased with his accomplishment, was far more grateful for the millions that this transaction would contribute to his own personal gain than he was the wall. However, he was most proud of something else—his secret document. Unbeknownst to the three leaders, this priceless document was placed in the safe at the resort. Murt took solace in knowing the portal was the twist in the deal that would make him a true hero of the American people. The document was safely tucked away at Par La Mer, and he was sure that he had outsmarted them all.

He motioned to the highly classified contents of the briefcase. "I provide you with access to this, my friends." He watched the leaders' expressions as they looked on. "This is my reassurance of our comradery. It serves to reinforce our agreement to never again allow war or discourse to divide our respective countries."

Petrov again exchanged glances with Mahdavi and Chang as a sharp smile invaded the corners of his mouth. Slowly and deliberately he raised his eyes until his gaze locked on Murt's. His ominous countenance vanished.

"You have done well, my friend," Petrov acknowledged. He closed the briefcase and slowly stood to his feet. "It has been far more than a pleasure to assist your great country in meeting its domestic needs and in helping you personally, my comrade. Unfortunately, however, due to the clandestine nature of this exchange, I think it best if we all agree to successfully conclude this settlement. I will contact you soon."

Swiftly, the three leaders headed toward the exit door of the dim conference room as the president followed.

"... and President Murt..." Petrov coldly spoke as he unexpectedly turned to face the president of the United States. "God-Bless-America."

∞∞∞∞∞∞∞∞∞∞∞

The call came in a week later.

It came to the private presidential line of Nadold P. Murt

at 3:00 a.m. Russian President Petrov, armed in full arrogance, made it.

"Mr. President," he growled. "I thought it only fair that I speak with you before I complete my gift to you and your American people."

The president turned on his side and squinted at the time on the digital clock.

"Yes, Petrov, why that's very kind of you," Murt responded groggily. He was more perplexed with the time of night than the ominous nature of the call.

"But why are you calling me directly at these hours, and what gift are you speaking of? I thought we agreed never to speak of our arrangement again, especially on these lines."

Petrov chuckled sarcastically. "Surely, your intelligence agencies don't surveil their own leader. However, I wanted to call you personally," he continued aloofly. "Especially as this may be the very last time you have the honor of speaking with me...you imbecile."

Murt paused. "Imbecile?" He sat up, shifting the receiver to his other ear. He had never been insulted by his new-found friend and ally.

"Did I hear you correctly?"

"Yes," Petrov slowly spoke. "I am joined here in my great country by both Mahdavi and Chang. We want to thank you for allowing us to box you in like the dirty rats that you Americans are."

"Excuse me?" Murt returned. "Did I just hear you correctly?"

"I am quite certain that you heard me correctly, President Murt," said Petrov. "Unfortunately, I must confess that I have been a bit dishonest with you. I had a much higher regard for President Oduya, whom you so strategically disgraced during his term. I only supported you because I knew that if the Democratic candidate Clemens had won the election, I would never have had this opportunity."

Murt threw back the covers and stood up, fully awake.

"You listen here!" he interjected as an angry color flushed his face.

"No!" Petrov snarled. "You listen! I have no respect for a man that would turn on his own people so willingly. What will they do when they find out that you have betrayed them and all for the sake of financial gain?"

"Well, we...we had a deal!" Murt stuttered. He could hear the two other leaders mocking him during the call.

"Thank you for America's nuclear codes. They have been disabled," said Petrov, chuckling coldly before terminating the call.

Murt panicked. Only months ago, he had become the most powerful leader of the free world. Now his plans were foiled. He was a sitting duck, along with millions of Americans who entrusted their safety and security to him. However, as many had thought, and just as Murt had shown them throughout his campaign, he was a savvy businessman. He always had a counterplan to get them before they could get him. And so, he did—but how could he use it now? His plan was hundreds of miles away at Par La Mer.

His new-found alliance included the dismantling of the missile defense system, and no missiles were aimed in the direction of his once-again enemies. The 3:00 a.m. phone call had caught him off guard. There was not enough time to make it to the secret document at Par La Mer, which could change everything. He would not be able to change the course of events as he had planned, and no matter how good his intentions, he couldn't right this wrong.

Nadold P. Murt quietly gathered his family, and they all returned to bed that night in a nuclear-proof room of the White House. Not wanting to accept the destruction that he knew he would awake to the next morning, he prayed that the portal would be discovered, yet still failed to warn the American people. He knew it would appear that he had betrayed his oath as the president of the United States of America, and that he had allowed World War III on a trusting and unsuspecting country without a single ally to come to her rescue. Murt wasn't sure if the truth would ever be discovered at Par La Mer. All he could hope for was that someday it would.

The sun rose the next morning on a new era. That day, in American history, would be recorded as the **_Annihilation,_** an American tragedy that over one thousand years later would lead to the initiation of... *the Righting Wars.*

Chapter 3∞
Little Warriors—Back to the future

3022 AD

Maya Pense knew the day she laid eyes on the tiny baby girl that there was something special about her. Maya's husband of ten years, Alfred, picked up on it too, despite the many hours he was required to work away from home. She marveled at how he made the most of his time with little Piper, perhaps as much as she admired him for his promotion to brigadier general in the Mission Marine Corps. His ranking was unheard of as no Sunz in the history of the Jenroe administration had ever attained this level, and no one had since.

The Penses, both Sunz, had never bore children of their own. However, Maya Pense was a strongly religious woman and truly believed that Piper was a gift from God. Furthermore, she could not bear the thought of Jenroe's medical mission coming in and taking a child of her own away just because of the physical appearance. So, they loved Piper with all they had.

Six years had passed since the night she was delivered to them, and Maya and Alfred had immediately begun developing the special talents they noticed in the days and years following the night their daughter was delivered to them. Piper proved to be an exceptional child. She began speaking before she was a year old, and by the time she was two, Maya had taught her to fully read. By age five, Piper was self-taught and had learned several different languages. Knowing her daughter would not fit into a conventional education system, and on Alfred's insistence, Maya resorted to telling others her daughter was home schooled, and since Piper was far from needing academic instruction, Maya focused her instruction on teaching her daughter about God.

Often annoyed by her mother's tendency to turn every lesson into a religious sermon, Piper looked forward to her lessons with her father. Alfred Pense instilled in little Piper the art of self-defense. By the age of six, Piper was a highly proficient green belt in the Marine Corps martial arts program. He himself was a 6th degree black belt. He had trained her relentlessly from the time she was able to walk and was very proud of the skills displayed by the tiny child. "Rowe," he called her. It was a nickname that Piper very much liked and made her feel strong like a "Warrior" she would say as her dad prepared her to attain the next level in her training program.

The day finally came, however, that Maya Pense discovered what was truly special about Piper.

"Rowe, have you finished your lesson?" Maya asked as she peered into the bedroom where Piper worked each day.

Already, at the age of six, she had mastered highly complicated mathematical and scientific concepts. Maya was amazed at the level of genius the child displayed, especially when the social belief instilled by the Jenroe administration was that the Sunzes were a genetic anomaly and such a level of genius would be impossible.

"Yes, Mom, I'm almost done," Rowe replied, uneasy with her mom's sudden entrance into the room.

This was not the first time Maya had experienced Rowe acting secretively. She wasn't sure how to react to the child's behavior as her daughter had always been such a good child. It was during these times that she would provide Rowe with the same spiritual guidance she herself had received as a child. Maya had come from a very religious family, and although Alfred did not display the same level of faith and spirituality with which she had been raised, they both tried to strongly instill Maya's goodness in Rowe.

"What's going on in here, Rowe?" Maya suspiciously probed as she caught sight of a bright, glowing light emanating from the closet.

Rowe did not respond. She stared at her mother and gazed back and forth from her closet to her mom.

"Rowe, you were told to write a short story, and did you read those Bible verses I assigned you? How much have you completed?"

"It's all done, Mother," Rowe softly replied, as her gaze continued to ping-pong back and forth between her mother and the closet door.

Maya reached for the paper directly in front of Rowe and gasped at what she read.

"The Initiation," was the title of the short story the six-year-old had written. It was all about overthrowing the Jenroes and the Missions.

"Rowe, you can't write such things!"

The bright light emanating from the crack in the closet grew brighter as the nervous child in front of her appeared anxiously distracted. Maya stepped toward the closet door.

"What's in there, Rowe?"

"Mama, no!" Rowe suddenly blurted out. "Don't go in there."

Just as Maya was about to open the closet door, she paused. "What is going on, Piper?" she asked with concern.

Rowe dropped her gaze, then slowly looked up at her mother. She knew when her mom called her by her real name, it usually meant trouble. She struggled to find the right words to explain, but she was sure her mom wouldn't believe her. However, she could never lie to her. She knew she had to tell the truth...

∞∞∞∞∞∞∞∞∞∞

The mysterious woman sat alone in a dark, quiet room. She meditated deeply. Engrossed in a trance-like state, she searched her mind for the existence of others. Of them all, Rowe was the youngest to be discovered. The woman had been a part of Rowe's life for as long as the little girl could remember.

27

However, Rowe did not know her true identity. One day, she would. One day, all of the children would meet, and one day, they would come together. She had now discovered six of the children. She knew that the privileged child was being hidden and would be difficult to reach, but the seventh child was an anomaly. She knew this child was out there, she could feel it... but why couldn't she see it?

∞∞∞∞∞∞∞∞∞∞∞

"I'm waiting, young lady!" Maya demanded with a stony expression.

"I'm...I...don't think...I mean...you won't believe me." Rowe nervously stuttered.

"Piper Sparrow!" Maya retorted. "You better tell me this very moment what's going on in that closet. And I also want to know what it has to do with this inappropriate story you just wrote."

"Okay, Mom," she softly replied with a deep sigh. "Here goes. The light is a portal that takes you to the story."

"It does *what?*" Maya immediately regretted her tone when she startled her little girl.

"Oh, honey, I'm sorry," said Maya. "I didn't mean to

scare you, but I'm not sure I heard you correctly. Did you say…"

"Yes, Mom…" Rowe interrupted as she spoke slowly and deliberately looking her mom directly in the eyes. "The light is a portal that takes you to my story. If you go in there, you live the story."

"Rowe, this can't be true." Maya softly chided. "You have to stop playing make-believe. What have we taught you about honesty?"

Rowe did not respond and dropped her gaze to the floor. Maya raised her voice.

"Piper Sparrow, I am speaking to you! You will look at me when I speak to you! Do you understand me?"

"Yes, Mom," Rowe answered as the tears slowly began to stream down her cheeks, "but…"

"But nothing, young lady!" said Maya. "Where would you get such a story? Now, I am not sure what you have been reading but…"

Maya stopped speaking mid-sentence as the glowing light illuminated the entire room. Her heart pounded. As each second passed, it occurred to her that Rowe could be telling the truth.

But that's impossible.

She slowly walked toward the closet. Suddenly, Rowe leaped from the bed and flung her arms desperately around her waist.

"Don't go in there, Mommy! Please, don't go in there!"

Maya was confused. She had only known her daughter to be honest, and Rowe had never played make-believe to the point of tears. As the tiny little arms gripped her fiercely, she could feel Rowe tremble violently. Confusion and fear grew in Maya. The little girl attached to her waist looked up at her with her face covered in tears. Maya stared back at Rowe, struggling to understand the sudden change in her behavior.

"Rowe, you are shaking, and you're scaring me," Maya whispered in an attempt to calm her.

"It's true, Mama. I've done it before…many times," Rowe said as she struggled to catch her breath. "I've changed our story."

Maya froze. "What do you mean you've changed our story, Rowe? What makes you think you can change our story?"

"The first time I did it was when I was four, and dad was fighting to move up in ranks. I wrote the story, and he became a brigadier general."

"How…how… did you?" Maya asked as she continued to

stare at Rowe in awe.

"I learned that if I write these stories, and I go through the portal, they can really happen. My stories will come true. They don't always happen exactly as I write them. Sometimes, I have to decide the ending, and I have to make the ending happen."

"This is too much, Rowe," said Maya, feeling weak. You do understand why this is very hard for Mommy to believe?"

"But I did, Mommy! I helped Daddy!" Rowe protested. Maya could see that the child was getting increasingly upset and shaking all the more. Whether or not the story was make-believe, there was definitely something going on in that closet that Rowe was trying to protect her from.

"Okay, sweetie, calm down, and stop crying. Now, there is something going on in that closet. I have to see what it is, for both my safety and yours. So, let me check it out, and then we can talk about this calmly."

"No, Mommy, please!" Rowe softly pleaded as tears continued to stream down her face. "Don't go in there. I promise. I will show you. Just don't go near the portal."

As baffled and confused as Maya was, she suddenly realized that there might be some truth to what the child was saying. She knew she had to listen.

"How did you help your father, Rowe? How did you write a story and then decide the ending? Tell me, Rowe!"

Rowe's eyes were completely swollen and filled with tears as she slowly raised her head to stare her mother directly in the eyes. Maya's heart began to break as she clearly saw the pain in the eyes of her little girl.

"In that story, no one could see color, Mama. They had no idea he was brown. So, I didn't have to change the ending."

Maya embraced her tightly, fighting back tears of her own. *Why should a small child have to carry around so much weight and pain?*

"It's going to be okay, Rowe." She gently stroked her daughter's hair. "Things will change someday, and something tells me you are going to be instrumental in that change."

She tipped Rowe's chin up and looked at her gravely. "But you can't write stories that change our circumstances. It is what it is. So, for now, no more make-believe stories. Do you understand me?"

"They are not make-believe, Mom," sobbed Rowe as she pulled away and crumpled up the pages of her story.

Slowly, the light coming from the closet vanished. Maya slumped onto the bed and stared in disbelief.

"See, Mom, if I destroy it before anything happens, the story goes away, but if I destroy it after the ending. There's no turning back."

"Dear Lord!" Maya gasped. *She's telling the truth.*

∞∞∞∞∞∞∞∞∞∞

As the day progressed, a thick blanket of stillness and silence engulfed the Pense home. While in her tenth rotation of scrubbing the kitchen countertops, the creaking of the door caused Maya to jump, signaling to Alfred Pense that something was off. He was an imposing figure standing in the doorway, handsome and appearing far younger than his middle-age years. Fairly tall, with broad shoulders and a muscular build, he accredited his militia career for his long-held youthful appearance.

Tonight, it was silence, along with the pleasant aroma of sweet potato pie that greeted him at the door. Maya did not turn to him but steadily busied herself with cleaning and setting the table, causing Alfred's sense of uneasiness to grow.

"Maya?" His eyes narrowed. "What's wrong, sweet heart?" For a moment, she failed to respond. When she faced him, the tears that covered her face were an obvious omen. The shaking plate she held crashed to the floor.

"Dear God, woman!" Alfred reacted. "I've only been gone eight hours!"

"I… I know." Maya nervously replied as she immediately kneeled to clear the broken glass.

"No, no." Alfred gently grabbed her wrist as he kneeled down beside his wife. "No, Maya, you're going to cut yourself. Here," he gestured, "Sit at the table. I'll get that while you tell me what in the world is going on."

Shakily, Maya sat at the table upon Alfred's insistence, while he cleared the broken shards.

"Is Rowe okay?" he nervously asked.

"Yes," she feverishly nodded.

"What, then? Why are you acting like this?"

"Lower your voice!" Maya anxiously whispered as she glared at the door of their daughter's room. "We need to talk."

Confused, Alfred slowly lowered himself to the table in a chair adjacent to her.

"Okay," he replied. "Just calm down. I'm sure whatever it is, we can fix it."

"I'm not so sure. Can you fix *this?*" she asked sarcastically, tossing Rowe's crumpled story on the table.

Alfred was confused. He reached for the paper on the table. "What's this?"

"No!" Maya yelled as she blocked his reach.

"What is this then, Maya?" he asked, his patience diminishing. "I need you to explain!"

"It's a story, Alfred," Maya sobbed. "A story about overthrowing the Jenroe administration—and our daughter wrote it!"

Alfred abruptly pushed back his chair, springing to his feet.

"Well, did you tell her she can't do that?" Beads of sweat formed on his forehead.

"Of course, I did," Maya snapped. "But that's not all. "Some kind of light appeared in her closet...and, well... she swears it's a place she can go to make her story come true."

Fear gripped at Alfred and his chest tightened.

Maya stood and went to him, gripping his arm and searching his eyes. "I don't know whether to believe her or not, but I saw the light myself!"

She shook his arm.

"Alfred, are you listening to me? I saw it, and when she crumpled this paper up, it went away."

"Well, believe her!" Alfred abruptly blurted out.

"Wh...what?" Maya said. "What did you say?"

Suddenly, silence fell upon the room. Maya Pense sat back down and gazed at her husband in shock. Slowly, Alfred lowered himself back in the chair. He softly grasped her hand.

"I said believe her, Maya. She's not lying," he spoke gently. "She has a gift."

"A gift?" Maya whispered in disbelief.

"There's a whole lot more to it," Alfred continued. "She can do exactly what she told you and then some, and it's very dangerous."

Suddenly, Maya started to cry. "I don't understand. How...?"

"Maya, we must never share this with anyone," Alfred interrupted, his voice urgent. "Rowe must never use this gift. They could take her away from us." Maya, in all her shock, finally realized her husband did not seem at all surprised to hear what had transpired with Rowe that morning.

"Alfred, is there something you're not telling me?"

"There are others, Maya. These children are generally born with a birthmark that designates them as what we now call *Righters*. It is believed that their abilities are a chance occurrence, some kind sequela from the undetectable nuclear emissions that still exist in the soil from the war over a thousand years ago, but we are not sure. It's a secret government operation. When the children are identified based on the birthmark, they are taken away. No one, not even I, know exactly where they place these children. We just know it's somewhere in Exilium. Rowe doesn't have an obvious mark, and there may be more like her."

"It's on her inner thigh." Maya slowly whispered.

"I know," said Alfred. "I saw it years ago when she was in diapers. When I was appointed brigadier general and received clearance to what made me privy to this operation, I remembered the mark, and my sole purpose since then has been to protect Rowe."

"Protect her from what, Alfred?" Maya said, angrily.

"How dangerous is this, and why did you hide it from me? You should have told me, Alfred!"

"I didn't tell you because I didn't want to put you at risk.

This is very dangerous, Maya, why do you think I insisted on home schooling? Think about it, Maya. It would have only made you more anxious and caused worry. If I had to do it all over again, I wouldn't change a thing."

"Well, that's not for you to decide, Alfred Pense! I am not some frail flower that you have to protect. Now, you had better tell me all you know about this, and tell me now. I have been in the dark far too long!"

Alfred paused and let out a deep sigh.

"You're right, Maya," he said. "You are strong, and it is time I tell you what I know."

Alfred paused again and looked deeply at his wife.

"The first Righter we know of was discovered centuries ago during early Jenroe rule. The gift was discovered when the young man was only a child. The government originally wanted to use his ability as part of the militia. He was referred to as a Righter for many reasons. The obvious is the play on words based on his ability to re-write or change history, but also because the original plan was for him to right a centuries-old wrong and change the outcome of the election of 2016, ultimately saving the United States of America from World War III. However, the

Jenroes didn't just want him to save America, they wanted the young man to completely re-write history, giving the Jenroes complete world domination."

Maya nodded, slowly absorbing her husband's words.

"Unfortunately," Alfred continued, "they never accomplished changing America's history. The young man was born and raised in the area that we live in today. Our territory, Righting, was named after him. As soon as he became an adult, on his 18th birthday, he revealed his opposition to the Jenroe regime and went completely rogue. The military scientists believe these children are the most dangerous once they enter adulthood. If they are caught writing a story, they are deemed an official Righter and are subject to annihilation by the Jenroe regime.

"I don't have much more information than that due to the classified nature of the file, but whatever else happened to the young man, Maya, ultimately, the Jenroe regime annihilated him because he was seen as a direct threat to the government. Not long after that, the government began searching for Righters. Soon they began to notice the pattern of the mark. They put out a call for parents to bring in all children who displayed the mark. They did not explain to parents why, and hundreds of parents turned their children over. These children were taken away from their families and placed in Exilium. In the past, they were slaughtered. This is what the classified files refer to as the Great Gathering, but it was removed from the history books. Since this gathering, all children born with the mark are taken away, and I won't allow them to take Rowe."

"How do we assure her safety?" Maya demanded. "Tell me, Alfred, how do we protect our child?"

"Right now, Maya, she's only six. We can keep her from writing or from anyone finding out about her gift, but she won't be six forever. This is why I train her so seriously. Someday she will have a mind of her own and will make decisions for herself. If she's writing these types of stories now, what do you think is going to happen in the future? She already sees the injustices of the Jenroe administration at six years old. God help us when she's older. She may someday be in for the fight of her life."

"We have to talk to her now, Alfred," Maya pleaded.

Suddenly, the creaking of the door revealed tiny Piper Sparrow. "I'm sorry, Papa. I won't write any more stories," she softly spoke as she lowered her eyes.

Alfred and Maya anxiously traded glances as they turned

to look at their scared little girl standing in the doorway. It was suddenly clear to them that she had no real understanding of her capabilities.

"It's okay, sweetie," Alfred reassured her as he and his wife embraced their beautiful and now vulnerable little girl. "Just no more stories and no one, absolutely no one, can know about this, or they could take you away from Mommy and Daddy. Do you understand?"

"Yes, Papa." Rowe promised. "No more stories."

∞∞∞∞∞∞∞∞∞∞

The next morning, the sun peered through the blinds of the Pense home while Maya busied herself preparing the morning coffee. Still attempting to process yesterday's heavy events, she was relieved to see Rowe sleeping soundly, but suddenly remembered that today was a government-mandated visitation day.

"Is she up yet?" Alfred asked, entering the kitchen.

"No, not yet," Maya anxiously responded as she scurried to unload the dishwasher. "After everything that happened yesterday, I completely forgot about her visit with the Sparrows. I have to hurry and get dressed. I can't be the reason she's late."

Alfred clearly noticed that Maya was overwhelmed and very worried about Rowe.

"Maya, your hands are shaking. Calm…"

Before Alfred could finish his sentence the glass bowl that Maya was putting away slipped from her hand and crashed to pieces on the floor. A soft whimper escaped Maya's lungs. She leaned against the kitchen counter to collect herself.

"This is becoming a habit," Alfred chuckled. "Come, sit down, Maya," he coaxed as he guided her to the kitchen chair. "It's going to be okay. I'll clean this up, and I'll take Rowe to her visit with the Sparrows."

"Are you sure?"

"Yes, I'm sure," Alfred said and smiled. "I don't have anything special going on at Righting Court this morning that's more important than you, and I could use the ride and some time with my daughter."

"You're such a wonderful husband and father," Maya whispered.

"I would be nothing without you," Alfred replied as he delivered a soft kiss to her forehead.

"I'm going to go get her up and dressed," said Maya.

"She'll be ready to go in a few minutes."

∞∞∞∞∞∞∞∞∞∞∞

As Alfred absorbed himself in the morning paper, the clinging of Rowe's spoon against the cereal bowl was the only noise in the home.

"Stop stuffing your mouth, young lady," Maya scolded as she returned to the kitchen to see them off.

"I'm ready, Papa!" Rowe said as she gulped down her final scoop of cereal and jumped to her feet.

"Well, you seem really excited," said Maya. "They must have special plans for you today."

"Sort of," Rowe gushed. "They have a pool, and Keelie and I are going swimming!"

"Oh, that sounds fun," said Alfred. "What about your brother, Patton? I never hear you say much about him."

Suddenly Rowe's smile vanished. She quickly slumped back in her chair. Confused by her sudden and dramatic mood change, Alfred peered above his black-framed reading glasses. He started to speak, but Maya beat him to it.

"What's wrong, Rowe? Is there something you want to tell us before you go to the Sparrows?"

"No, Mommy," she softly replied. "But…"

"But what, Rowe?" asked Maya. "You know you can talk to us about anything."

"Well, sometimes I don't understand why God gave me two mommies and two papas.

"I told you," Alfred interjected. "It's because you're special. We've always made sure you knew that."

"Well, that is not what Patton says," Rowe replied.

Maya frowned. "What do you mean?"

Rowe silently fidgeted with her spoon, annoyingly clanging it against the cereal bowl.

"Exactly what does Patton say?" Alfred asked.

"Patton says it's because I'm brown. He says Jana and Philmore didn't want me to live there because I'm brown. He calls me mud, too, Papa. He's mean to me sometimes."

"Oh, sweetie, Patton's just being childish," Maya responded.

"Well, he's the same age as me!" Rowe blurted out. "And Jana says we're twins."

"Yes, you are," said Alfred.

"Well, how can he live in Imperium with my other

mommy and papa, and I can't.

Maya and Alfred nervously traded glances. They had never considered that Rowe might someday be unhappy in their home, and they were fearful of where her questions would take them.

"Is that what you want?" Maya calmly asked. "Do you want to live with the Sparrows?"

"No, Mommy," Rowe replied. "I just want to live closer to Keelie. Why can't we all move to Imperium?"

Silence invaded the room. Maya and Alfred knew the day would come when Rowe would begin to ask questions, but they never expected it would be this soon. Although she was only six years old, they were very conscious of her high level of intelligence and the time had come to retire the excuse that her situation was because "she was special."

"Patton must be right," Rowe finally spoke. "It must be because I'm brown."

"No, Rowe. It's far more complicated than that and hard to explain to you now because you are so young," replied Alfred.

"There are many people like you, me, and your mother in this world, but life here in the United Missions is a little different."

"How is it different, Papa?"

"Well, it all started a long time ago, Rowe. Over a thousand years ago, this country was called the United States of America, and it had fifty territories called states."

"Wow, that sounds really big, Papa."

"It was really big," replied Alfred. "I can't even imagine that many people in one country."

"It was a beautiful country, too!" Maya interjected. "The best thing was that everyone lived together. There was no separation of where you could live."

"What happened to the old country, Papa?" asked Rowe. "Why did it change?"

Alfred pulled her onto his lap.

"The old America was the greatest and the richest country in the world, Rowe. However, over a thousand year ago, many Americans were hurting. They were struggling to pay bills and eat. Many couldn't get jobs. They were also having great difficulty getting basic health care, and many of them wanted a change. People were feeling forgotten and mistreated—especially the Palers. That was the year they voted Nadold P. Murt as the 45th president of the United States of America."

"That's a funny name," Rowe laughed.

"Yea, it is sort of funny," Alfred chuckled. "However, what happened after Murt became president was very serious. It is a time in our history referred to as the Annihilation. Murt became president because the American people were angry, and he made many promises—some good and some bad—but ultimately, he betrayed the American people and changed this country forever."

"What did he do?" Rowe asked.

"Well, that's really complicated, and you will get to that in your history lessons. Basically, he started a war that destroyed America. Most Americans perished horribly. It took hundreds of years for Americans to begin to rebuild, and it was not long before the dictatorship of the Jenroes stepped in and changed everything. The Jenroe family has controlled America for a very long time, and there has not been a truly fair election since the repeal of the XXII amendment over 500 years ago."

Maya chuckled. "She has no idea what an amendment is Alfred. We have not studied that yet."

"Yes, I do, Mommy," Rowe replied. "I read ahead of you sometimes."

"Well, good for you," said Alfred. "So, I guess you understand that the presidency is now a role that is passed down through the Jenroe family, although elections continue to be held every four years. Unfortunately, none of us living can remember a time when the country's leader did not carry the surname of Jenroe."

"Actually, the first Jenroes to rule were pretty fair," said Maya.

"How would you know that, Mommy?"

"Well, I guess we can assume it," explained Maya. "because even though all the territories existed, Americans were allowed to live wherever they wanted. Granted, wealth was not equally dispersed, but the dream of life, liberty, and pursuit of happiness still existed in the hearts and the future plans of many."

"When did it all change?" Rowe asked.

"Well, young lady," said Maya, standing up, "I think you and your daddy better continue this conversation later, or you'll be late getting to the Sparrows."

Alfred kissed his wife and gave her a reassuring look before he and Rowe walked out the door to the car. Rowe was quiet for a while as the miles passed on their drive to Imperium, but Alfred knew she was thinking deeply, and he waited. It wasn't until they drove through the Metisse territory that Rowe spoke again.

"So, when did things change, Daddy? When did they stop letting us live wherever we want?"

"In 2520," Alfred explained, pointing out the window. "See the Metisse territory there?" The Jenroe Regime separated the territories based on race because the Metisse population became what the old Americans referred to as the true melting pot. The Metisse people had no identifiable racial identity. They were ambiguous due to the racial mixing that took place when Americans were trying to rebuild and survive after the war. It turned out that there were no true racially pure Americans. Actually, we are all Metisse."

"Well, Papa, if we are all Metisse," Rowe asked, as if confused, "then why are some of us called Sunz and others called Paler?"

Alfred's hands tightened on the steering wheel. He knew this would be the hardest question to answer. Maybe he had shared enough for today, although her curiosity and knowledge made him proud. He looked over at Rowe as she gazed intently, waiting, then sighed heavily, knowing she wouldn't get out of the car without an answer.

"Unfortunately, every now and then a Paler or a Sunz can be born in any of the three races," he explained as he slowly pulled into the Sparrow's driveway. "It's Jenroe law that they be removed and placed in a home based on their physical characteristics."

Rowe listened as she stared at the Sparrow's ostentatious home. New and mixed feelings stirred within her.

Alfred parked the car and reached over to gently touch his daughter's smooth cheek as she turned to look back at him. "Rowe, your skin is brown because you are a Sunz, and all Sunzes are mandated by law to reside in the territory of Righting. The Sparrows have fair skin and they are Palers. They are mandated to reside in the territory of Imperium. That is why you were taken from the Sparrow home and given to me and your mom."

Alfred reached in the back for her bag. "Rowe, Patton is wrong. Jana and Phil love you very much, but just like us, they have to follow the law. They trusted Maya and me to love and to raise you, and we were blessed to receive you."

Alfred kissed his daughter goodbye.

Chapter 4 ∞
The Drive to Imperium—

10 years later

Piper Sparrow heard the sizzle of bacon coming from the kitchen as the tempting aroma roused her from a deep sleep. It had been a late night of cramming for final exams. Although it was summer, her home school regimen was year-round and her instructor, Maya Pense, took no pity on her when it came to academics.

"College opportunities for you are already limited, Rowe," her mother would preach. "You're a Sunz, so you must be the best to get accepted with the best."

The good news was that home school had already afforded Rowe the opportunity of earning her bachelor's degree in advanced technology. Graduation was approaching, and she would graduate with her high school diploma and her college degree simultaneously. Although Alfred discouraged Maya from letting Rowe advance so far above her level, Maya refused to stifle the exceptional intellect that Rowe displayed early on. She was amazed at how easily Rowe solved the most complex mathematical calculations and often caught her reading books that were well beyond her years. Even at six years old, Rowe understood themes embedded in some of the greatest classics. Maya and Alfred very much looked forward to Rowe getting accepted into one of the best graduate schools, but they worried about her being just 16.

"Rowe, it's time to get up and get dressed," Maya scolded as she stood in the doorway drying her hands on a dish towel. "You don't want to keep the Sparrows waiting."

"Okay, Mom," Rowe grumbled as she attempted to stretch out of the sleep that she so desperately wanted to return to.

"Okay, young lady, I mean it!" Maya had her hands on her hips now. "Get up from there. Jana needs me to pick you up on time today, and I have to give them their court ordered time with you. Let's not forget, we have exams next week."

"Jana, Jana, Jana!" Rowe scoffed as she muffled her words with the covers drawn above her head. "It's always what Jana wants. Ugh!"

Frustrated, Rowe threw the covers aside and slowly

dragged herself out the bed. Moments later, she joined her parents at the breakfast table. She loved mornings when she woke to find her dad still there, sipping his coffee at the table and reading his morning briefs from his tablet.

"Good morning, sleepy head," Alfred Pense greeted his daughter, who now looked more like a young adult than a teenager. She had grown into a very beautiful young lady. The wiry coif on her head consumed her entire face forcing her to pull it back with a large band. He was very protective of Rowe, as she had no idea how physically beautiful she truly was. The mandatory visits with her biological family weighed heavily on her, and, unbeknownst to the Penses, they were affecting Rowe more than they knew.

Rowe poured a glass of orange juice in silence.

"Smile, sunshine," said Alfred. "What's the melancholy look all about? I thought you might be excited about going to the Sparrow's today. Keelie will be there."

"I know," Rowe mumbled as she shrugged. She stared at her plate, flipping her bacon over and over with her fork."

Maya frowned. "Hey, that's your breakfast. Stop playing with it and eat up. You need your energy."

She and Alfred traded glances. They could clearly see something was going on with Rowe.

"You want to talk about it, sweetie?" Alfred asked.

Rowe sat in silence. She glanced at her mom as if she were unsure about speaking in front of her.

"Well, do you want me to leave the room?" Maya responded, raising her eyebrows. She hoped her expression didn't hint of her hurt feelings.

"Oh, no, Mom, of course not," said Rowe. "It's just… well… do I have to go today?"

Maya and Alfred traded glances again. In their hearts, they had known this day would come, but they had not expected it so soon.

"Yes, young lady, you have to go," Maya responded as she cleared the breakfast dishes. "You know it's the law. We can't keep you from your biological family if we wish to keep you with us. That's been the agreement for 16 years, and for 16 years you have visited them once a month. What would Keelie say, anyway? I thought you looked forward to seeing your sister."

"Well, Keelie's not always there! Ever since she married into that family, I don't see her much anymore, and Patton doesn't say much to me. He just points out how we're twins and look nothing alike. I don't like it over there, Mom. Jana is so aloof, and Phil…well, he's a goofball. He walks around like nothing has happened. For God's sake, I'm their child too! And I was taken away because of what? Because of my skin color? And that's acceptable to those people? I don't want to be around them! Mom, you raised me well. Philmore and Jana claim to believe and have faith in God…What a bunch of hypocrites. You're my real mother! You know what true faith is. Isn't there some kind of verse that condemns them to hell for being such hypocrites?"

"That's enough, young lady!" Alfred barked. "The Sparrows have been nothing but kind to you, and they have not only shown it over 16 years of your life, but they have voiced their love and concern for you as well."

"Oh, I don't care what they say," continued Rowe, pushing away her plate. "They never loved me. They are pretenders as far as I am concerned!"

"Rowe, please!" Maya begged. "Have you forgotten our lessons on forgiveness? Remember, we are all affected by this, even the Sparrows. You have to forgive them, Rowe. They never caused you any harm. If you don't at least try to see the good in your family, that anger you harbor will destroy you."

"I am not harboring anger!" Rowe yelled. "I just don't want to go on this stupid visit again. You have no idea how it is there…"

As Rowe continued on her diatribe, Maya's mind drifted off to a time when she was not much older than her daughter and had similar feelings. She knew the pain and price of that path, but she didn't know how to make Rowe understand. All she could do was pray for her daughter.

By the time Rowe finished, she had herself completely in tears. Alfred and Maya felt powerless. They couldn't change the law, and they didn't want to lose their only child.

"Unfortunately, sweet heart, you have to go," Alfred said softly but sternly. "Once you're 18, if you still feel this way, you don't have to see them. Who you spend your time with will be completely up to you."

He stood up from the table and walked over to give Maya a kiss. "I have to get going. Just make sure you get her there on time."

As he hugged Rowe goodbye, he felt her stiffen, and he left that morning feeling a deep dread. He knew this was just the beginning. Rowe's opinions of the world around her grew stronger each day. He wasn't sure if Maya's wisdom and persistent sharing about forgiveness and understanding were making any difference in the young woman that his daughter was developing into. All he could hope for was that someday Maya's goodness would resonate in her.

"Go on, Rowe," said Maya. "We need to leave in a half hour to miss the traffic."

Rowe exited the kitchen and went to her room to prepare for the visit with her biological family, completely unaware that her mother, who was dear to her heart, felt a sense of panic. However, with every sense of panic, Maya Pense did as she always did. She went off to her room to pray. Unbeknownst to Rowe, Maya also dreaded this visit, even though a small part of her looked forward to it.

∞∞∞∞∞∞∞∞∞∞

The drive to the Sparrow's home was about two hours from the Righting territory. Although both territories were very large, both families lived close to the borders of their respective territories. For the entire ride, Rowe found herself wishing that the trip was much further. Taking into account that Rowe wasn't exactly happy about her monthly visits, Maya took her time driving, but kept in mind being a minute late would violate the biological law.

As Rowe stared out the window, she couldn't help but drift into a state of wonder at how different life was now, compared to what she had learned from history. It was amazing to her that drive from one territory to another took so little time. Cars rarely traveled on the old interstate Highway system that had crumbled terribly due to the Jenroe administrations unwillingness to restore them.

Luckily innovation was not a scarcity. Over five hundred years ago the Interale better known as the Rale had been created. An intricate skyway transport system that accommodated all cars, and it was even more advanced today. Exits off the Rale onto the main highways within the territories connected directly to the roads getting everyone from point A to B, but unfortunately, they were highly guarded at several checkpoints by the Jenroe administration.

Militia guards were stationed at various check points directly on the Rales throughout the territories, as well as in many other top secret and unseen areas hovering above them. The

Airforce militia was placed to protect the no-fly zones. The early Jenroe administration established specific airspace zones throughout the territories to keep the Sunz and Metisse from traveling outside of the country—which was strictly prohibited. Luckily there were only two checkpoints between Righting and Imperium. Rowe cringed every time she and her mother encountered one of the zone checkpoints on the Rale, but she cringed even more to know that the militia of the Jenroe administration was very likely hovering above them—watching their every move.

However, the good news about the Rale was that cars could travel almost at the speed of jets. She wished Maya would slow down, because no matter how crumbled the landscape appeared below, the mountains and the hills were beautiful to her, and only got more beautiful the closer they traveled toward Imperium. Not many cars were traveling today, and she was in no rush to get to the Sparrows.

Maya's mind wandered. When they neared Imperium, she rolled down her window. She always enjoyed this part of the ride that transitioned from the countryside of Righting to the Imperium territory. She breathed in the scent of the fresh flowers that cascaded over the landscape. Entering Imperium was like transitioning into another world. Only Palers resided in Imperium, and their houses looked like castles. Rowe's voice broke the silence.

"How long has it been like this, Mom?"

"What do you mean?"

"I mean, this place is amazing. How long did it take to build all of this?" Rowe's gaze passed over the countryside.

Maya began to answer, but then her thoughts drifted off again. It had been during these last two decades that the Jenroe administration had changed Imperium so drastically. It was now designated as the territory for the rich and wealthy Palers. The entire landscape was majestic. Towering and elegant buildings dotted the landscape. They were far and beyond anything seen in the Righting territory. Extravagant architecture in both the residential and commercial areas of Imperium reflected that this was truly the capitol of the country.

"Mom...*Mom?*" Rowe called out. "I asked you a question. How long did it take to build all of this?"

"Well, hundreds of years, I suppose," Maya replied, "but the territories were only fully established in the last two decades…I mean, with these big, beautiful buildings and all the advanced technology."

"What are those buildings for?" Rowe asked, pointing to several structures that loomed over the rest.

"Oh, those?" replied Maya. "Those are the mission headquarters. All of the high-level missions like the medical, politico, and law are here in Imperium."

"I wonder why *that* is?"

"Don't be so cynical, young lady," Maya reprimanded. "Yes, they do make good money here, and we may not have all of these fancy buildings and floating digital billboards in Righting, but God has more than blessed us with what we need to live comfortably."

Rowe rolled her eyes. She couldn't believe how naïve her mother was when it came to her God, and the Jenroe administration, and she couldn't believe that Maya considered any part of their situation a blessing. However, she wasn't brave enough to say it aloud to her mother, especially the part about her God.

"Well, I think it's unfair," Rowe said as she continued to stare out the window. Everyone knows that the majority of the government funding comes to Imperium. I remember Dad saying that we can be sure things aren't changing anytime soon." She turned and looked at Maya. "I just don't get how everyone can sit back and just allow this to continue."

"Well, Rowe, the truth is that many people do care," Maya corrected. "The trouble began with coercion and illegal voting practices dating back to the first Jenroes who took office. It didn't begin with our current President, Jeremy Jenroe. Many years ago, the Jenroes strategically set up territories and put individuals in power that would ensure their re-election each term."

"How did they do that?" Rowe scoffed. "It's not fair."

"Oh, Rowe," Maya replied. "It wasn't a new concept. The idea was derived from an ancient government practice referred to gerrymandering. The territories were set up in a manner that would guarantee a continued majority of the Droite Politica power. They control us locally by not allowing elections. Rather, they appoint Palers from the Droite Politica to the highest offices in all territories with the exception of Exilium."

"Does the Metisse territory look like this?" asked Rowe. "Heavens, no!" Maya replied. "It looks pretty much like Righting, just larger. There's far more Metisse than Palers and Sunz, so their territory is much larger."

"Is that why they are allowed to keep their Sunz children?" Rowe probed.

"Well, partially," replied Maya. Technically, the Metisse are many different races of people, but they appear racially ambiguous, so they can keep their Sunz children, but they can't keep the Palers. The Palers must go to Imperium."

"Palers get to keep Metisse children," said Rowe. "Why is that? Patton was allowed to stay with the Sparrows. He looks like a Metisse."

"Yes, he does," replied Maya, "but he's very ambiguous, racially. He could just as well say he's a Paler."

"I guess you're right," Rowe slowly replied. "But what about the Native lands and Exilium?"

Maya paused. Rowe had never asked her so many questions about their country. Other than what they discussed in her history lessons, she had never shown any curiosity as to what the other citizens looked like or what life was like outside of Imperium and Righting.

"Well, no one talks about the Native lands because we are forbidden to go there," Maya softly explained.

"Why?" Rowe persisted.

"We just are, Rowe," said Maya, feeling a hint of exasperation. "Those poor people have been through so much. The Natives suffered a great deal at the hands of the old government of this country called the United States. Years ago, after the annihilation and during Creed's rule, the Natives were provided with their own lands. A new constitution was implemented that provided the Natives with international protections, should their rights be infringed upon.

"Later, the original Jenroe administration signed a treaty granting that the Native lands not be disturbed, and that they could live freely in their designated territory without Jenroe interference. Surprisingly, the government has honored that agreement for many years now, but in the past, they broke many treaties and promises to the Natives. It's only a matter of time before they break it again."

"How do you know they haven't already broken promises to the natives?" Rowe asked. "No one is allowed to go to the Native's land, and no one truly knows what goes on there."

"You have a point," said Maya, "but the wise mind their own business. I have chosen to live my life wisely, and so should you, young lady. I do believe that the Lord will protect the Natives. They have gone through enough."

"Well then, what about Exilium?" Rowe pressed. "You never answered my question about that territory."

"What about it, Rowe?" Maya snapped. "You should know that answer based on its name. It's where the exiled are sent. What more do you need to know?"

There was silence inside the car for quite some time before Rowe spoke again. She could clearly see she had upset her mother. Speaking of the territories was not easy for Maya.

"I'm sorry, Mom. I just wonder sometimes if the people in Exilium are taken care of."

"Well, unfortunately, Rowe," Maya replied, "those sent to Exilium have in some way defied the laws of their territory."

"So, they commit a crime, and they're just written off?" Rowe said, frowning.

"Well, the worst crime they can commit is to practice sedition," replied Maya. "There are other crimes, however, such as supporting a political party outside of what was mandated of them." "I guess that means only Metisse and Sunz are sent to Exilium," Rowe concluded. "I can't think of why a Paler would not support the Droite party. I mean, it benefits them."

"Well, you're wrong," Maya replied, matter-of-factly. "All Palers are not bad. The Sparrows are a perfect example. Though to many, Exilium may seem like the most dreaded place to live, they do a lot of great things there. There are orphanages that take care of children who have no parents, hospitals, and many religious institutions. Rebel Palers are sent there, too, along with Metisse and Sunz. They live and work together in Exilium. Many Palers and Sunz are there for defying the Droite Party of the Jenroe administration and supporting the Gauche Party of the Metisse."

Rowe glowered. "Well, don't worry. I won't get into another debate with you about the Sparrows, Mom. But don't you find it strange that the Metisse are mandated to support the Gauche Party? I mean, since the Natives are no threat, why don't they require that we all support Droite? Why have two politico parties at all? You and Dad are forced to support Droite, aren't you?"

"Yes, we are," Maya replied. "All citizens of the Righting territory must support the Droite Politico, or we will end up in Exilium. However, when you put the two smallest territories together, our votes outnumber the votes in the largest. It gives the appearance of a fair election, Rowe."

"Then why are you so content with living like this?" Rowe continued to probe. "I mean, you seem to like Righting. Why?"

"In Righting, we are all Sunz," replied Maya. "We are the least diverse territory racially, but the only territory that contains several classes of people. Many Sunz are very poor. Some of us are okay, like me and your father. We make do with what we have. However, there are many Sunz who are wealthy. They are not quite as wealthy as the folks in Imperium, but unfortunately, the wealthy Sunz are controlled by the Jenroe administration and appointed to low-level leadership positions in our territory.

"Righting leadership strongly supports the Droite Politica as a means of maintaining their wealth and their class standing. However, if any in the Righting middle class and poor desire to support the Gauche, they dare not. Most, if not all, Sunz vote Droite out of intimidation and fear of the mandate. Although we vary in our professions and class, we are not allowed to enter into the high-level missions. Those missions are reserved for Palers."

Rowe slumped in her seat and crossed her arms. "It seems to me that if everyone would just come together and stand up to our government, then we could change things. It's always going to be like this if we just sit idle and allow it. I just don't understand how this could happen."

"Unfortunately, dear," Maya replied, "it all begins with division. You have to find a way to divide people in order to conquer them. Although we don't speak of it often, what we are painfully aware of is that it all began with Nadold P. Murt, as your father and I first explained to you when you were small. He was the president who changed the state of America forever. Historically, although corrupt in in their tactics for maintaining rule, the Jenroe's have been fair leaders. However, the election of 3016 closely mirrored what the history books had taught about the election of 2016. Yet, everyone ignored all the hate being spewed throughout the elections by Jeremy Jenroe. Unfortunately, Americans were afraid to speak out, and we still are. It was easier for many to just ignore that Jenroe welcomed the support of Neo Nazi regimes of the extreme Droite Politica, and now, for the last 16 years, we have grown into a nation even more divided."

"Well, if you ask me, Exilium doesn't seem that bad," said Rowe. "They don't seem so divided there."

"It can be a really sad place to visit sometimes," Maya

replied with a sigh. "You know I volunteer there quite often. Their wages are low. Granted, they receive the lowest level mission jobs, but honestly, more peace exists in Exilium than any of the territories."

"Why do you think that's so?" asked Rowe.

"Because they need each other, Rowe, and there is nothing like needing one another to foster unity."

Rowe was asking too many questions for Maya. Her thoughts went back to that day years ago when she and Alfred discovered that Rowe possessed a power greater than any mandate the government could put forth. She knew that Rowe had no idea how dangerous her power truly was, and that it could change everything, but, just as she had done since the night her daughter was delivered to her—all Maya could do was pray.

∞∞∞∞∞∞∞∞∞∞

Rowe and Maya pulled up into the extravagant drive of the Sparrow family, nearing the highly guarded gates at the entrance of their home.

Although they encountered this scene each month when they made these visits, it was something Maya knew her daughter would never get used to. She cringed whenever the guards looked at her daughter as if she didn't belong. Each time they arrived, the guards relentlessly interrogated them. Surely it was obvious by now that her daughter was the child of the Sparrow family, ordered to maintain monthly biological visits. Worse than their questions were the humiliating routine searches. This visit was no different.

"Don't worry, Rowe," consoled Maya. "They're only doing their job."

Rowe didn't respond. She was quiet for the remainder of the drive as they wound down the long, gated road to the Sparrow mansion. Her face was turned toward the window, but Maya knew what was happening in her heart. This particular visit was upsetting her daughter more than any other.

She felt the tightness in her chest. *I hope she's not planning to fix this.* She thought, but she knew in her heart that Rowe had every intention of doing just that.

Chapter 5∞
THE FAMILY

Philmore Sparrow stood at the enormous double doors in the grand entrance to the Sparrow mansion as he eagerly greeted the arrival of his biological daughter and Maya Pense. Rowe enjoyed a silent chuckle as she watched her biological father awkwardly flail his arms as if directing them to the entrance of a home that she had visited a countless number of times.

Rowe's impression of him had always been that he was quite weird. Initially, she believed him to be fairly humorous, but as she grew older, his antics only irritated her. She surmised his behavior was more than likely an attempt to compensate for the cold aloof reception she always experienced from Jana. Unbeknownst to Rowe, Philmore secretly harbored shame that traced back to the night she was taken away from his wife. He blamed himself for not protecting his family and allowing the militia that accompanied the medical mission to take his daughter away. He felt like less than a man for allowing himself to be overpowered and beaten. Most of all, he harbored a deep resentment toward Jana for signing those papers prior to the birth of their twins, agreeing to give them up if either of them was born a Sunz.

Unfortunately, it didn't seem to make much difference knowing that the reason his wife readily signed that document was because she never thought one of her children would be born a Sunz. They both appeared to be of the pure Paler blood, although all Americans now tested 50-50 of each race with the exception of a small population of Americans who were of 2 to 10 percent Hispanic heritage or some other ethnicity.

It seemed to him that Jana had decided long ago she would feel no guilt for Piper's circumstances. Their child had been placed in a good home with good people. Perhaps she convinced herself that Piper would never be comfortable as a part of their family since she looked so different. Whatever it was, Philmore resented her for it. Why couldn't Jana see past her own daughter's skin color?

Philmore finished ushering in the car. He stood waiting in front of the house, which seemed stark and lifeless, except for a small movement at the foyer window no one noticed.

∞∞∞∞∞∞∞∞∞∞∞

Jana Sparrow sat her wine glass down and, ever so slightly, drew back the drapery of the floor-to-ceiling foyer window to peer out. She took a deep breath and watched Rowe hug Maya goodbye. Only she knew the depths of her internal struggle over what took place in her home years ago on that direful night. The only anesthetic she had to lessen her pain was her consumption of alcohol, a habit that tore daily at the fiber of her family.

Withstanding Piper's brown skin, her daughter's striking blue eyes and beautiful bone structure was that of her own, yet all she would allow herself to see each time she looked at Piper was Alfred and Maya Pense. It was too painful to think otherwise and far more painful to share her feelings with anyone other than herself.

As the door knob turned, she quickly turned and exited the room.

∞∞∞∞∞∞∞∞∞∞∞

Rowe followed Philmore through the ornate doorway and up the winding staircase.

"You can put your things in your room," instructed Philmore. "Your brother is in the media room. He's been looking forward to seeing you."

Rowe stared blankly at him. You've got to be kidding, she thought. But she resigned to play along. She dropped her things off in her room and headed toward the media center to join Patton. Secretly, she hoped he'd leave as soon as she entered the room. She wanted to be alone. This room was where she spent most of her time when visiting the Sparrow's home. Since Keelie moved out, having this time to herself was the only good part of the visits. Most of her time at the Penses involved some type of studying, and this room afforded her a mental escape. Furthermore, the people in Imperium were given access to real media. The networks in Righting were extremely limited due to government control.

As she walked into the media room, it took a few seconds for her eyes to adjust. It was dark, except for a bright light emanating from the enormous screen in the room and daintily lighted cup holders on the theater chairs. She could make out a figure slouched in one of the reclined seats.

The figure shifted.

"Oh, it's you," Patton said aloofly. He reached for his drink without looking her way.

She ignored his condescending attitude.

"What are you watching?" Rowe asked.

"Oh, nothing," He replied. "You can change it if you want to."

Rowe was surprised. For the first time in their lives, Patton didn't get up and leave the room when she entered. She flipped through the channels and suddenly burst into laughter at the funny site of a clown dancing on a stage.

Soon Patton's silence made her uneasy. She could sense his discomfort, too. It was becoming apparent that he had something to say. She decided she would ignore him and continue watching the show. Finally, his repeated glances got to her.

"What is it?" Rowe suddenly blurted.

Tension hung between them like a thick wall for several seconds, but before she could return to the show, Patton spoke up.

"How is it there?" he asked.

Rowe was confused. *He couldn't possibly be asking about Righting. He never has before.*

She wrinkled her brow. "Where?"

"There, replied Patton. "How is it to live in Righting?"

"Oh, it's fine. I have great parents, for the most part...Well, Mom can be a little overbearing at times. She's really into this Bible stuff. Always on me about forgiveness and seeing the good in others. She's constantly in my ear preaching, 'For if you forgive other people when they sin against you, your heavenly father will also forgive you...'"

"...but if you do not forgive others their sins," Patton suddenly joined in, "your heavenly Father will not forgive your sins."

Rowe was caught off guard. She suddenly regretted mocking her mother. She'd never have guessed Patton knew that Bible verse—or anything about the Bible, for that matter.

"Mathew 6, verses 14-15," Rowe whispered. "How did you know that?"

"Believe it or not," replied Patton, "Mom, used to say that same Bible verse all the time. I haven't heard her recite it in quite a while though." His voice trailed off and he looked down as he played with the straw in his drink.

All was quiet. For Rowe, it was an awkward moment. She detected a sense of sadness in Patton. More than that, she was taken aback at the thought of Jana and Maya having anything in common. Several moments passed. Maybe he had finally reached his limit of being alone with her. But to her surprise, he remained.

"Do you have friends?" Patton abruptly asked.

"Yea, but not many. My studies keep me busy."

"Well, what about school? Mom says you're graduating soon. How did that happen? We should have another year in school."

Rowe's annoyance bumped up a level. However, the thought that Patton might truly be making an effort to get to know her kept her in check.

"Well, yes," said Rowe. "Mom homeschools me, so I'll finish up a little early. I also finished my first four years of college. I guess the next step for me is grad school."

"*Grad* school?" Patton was incredulous. "You're only 16!"

Rowe didn't respond. She glared at him out of the corner of her eye then continued to watch the screen. Silence hovered between them once again, and Rowe was relieved that her brother was no longer prying.

"Well, at least Mom and Dad made sure you were placed in a good home," Patton suddenly blurted. "You know how those people can be."

Rowe turned to completely face him. "What do you mean those people? You mean my people? Our people? We all come from the same people! We just look different!"

"You see what I mean?" Patton shot back. "People like you have violent tendencies. It's because of too much melanin." He headed for the door. "Enjoy your visit!"

Rowe remained in the media room for the majority of her visit. It wasn't until dinner time that she joined the rest of the family. The Sparrow dinner table was fairly quiet. Rowe was a little disappointed as her older sister had not shown up. Keelie was the only member of the Sparrow family with whom she shared a bond. She usually joined them for dinner on Rowe's monthly visits. Unfortunately, Keelie's absence made way for more tension. Rowe hated it when Philmore and Jana attempted to make small talk with her.

"Piper, stop playing with your food and eat," Jana barked. "Maya will be here in a bit to pick you up, and I have an engagement."

Piper remained silent. Jana was not the best cook in the world, and her culinary skills paled in comparison to her mother's.

"Why do we eat the same meal every time I visit?" Rowe asked, pushing food around on her plate.

Jana took a large gulp of her tea and cleared her throat as the color rose to her cheeks.

"Well, Piper," Jana snapped, "Maya tells me it's your favorite meal, and as your mom..."

"You are *not* my mother!" Rowe coldly interjected.

"Young lady!" Jana retorted. "I *am* your mother, and you will not speak to me in that tone!"

"You are not my mom!" Rowe yelled again, "and I..."

"Enough!" Philmore interrupted. "You will not speak to your mother in that manner in this home, young lady."

Tears welled up in Rowe's eyes. She looked across the table at Patton and could clearly see he was enjoying every minute. As emotion and frustration overcame her, she stormed to her room, swiftly locking the door behind her.

Jana slowly stood, excusing herself from the dinner table. She headed towards the liquor cabinet.

"Oh, no, Jana." Philmore said gruffly. "Not today."

"Yes, today, Philmore!" Jana smirked as she gulped down half a glass of wine before he could get to her. "Today and every day."

"You have no idea what you are doing to this family," Philmore said as he grabbed ahold of her wrist. "We had a deal. No drinking on Piper's visits."

Jana ignored him. When he released her wrist, she poured herself a second glass. Philmore shook his head in disbelief. Neither of them noticed Patton who had gotten up from the table. He slowly walked toward his room, tears welling up in his eyes.

Across the hall, it was no surprise to Rowe that no one had followed her. She cried, sitting alone in the stark silence of the room. She was oblivious as to how the Sparrow family was being torn apart by the very situation she hated them for. It wasn't long before she felt saved by the ringing of the doorbell.

"Finally," she whispered. "Mom."

However, the voice that reverberated through the house was Keelie's and it quickly turned into a whisper. Rowe's first thought was to run out of the room to her sister, but she couldn't stomach another moment in the presence of the others. She decided it was best to let Keelie come to her. She was sure they were filling Keelie in on the events of dinner.

Just as Rowe suspected, when the whispering ceased, Keelie peered through the bedroom door. Like Rowe, Keelie had inherited Jana's striking blue eyes. Rowe took a deep breath. She felt a sense of warmth in Keelie that she never felt with any of the others.

"Hey, kiddo, want some company?" Keelie asked, smiling.

"Keelie!" Rowe sprang from the bed and embraced her sister.

"Hey, little one," Keelie replied, squeezing her tight, then holding her at arm's length to look at her. "Oh, well, you're not so little anymore. Look at you. You're more like an adult every time I see you. I think we're starting to look more alike." She smiled as she turned Rowe around so they both faced the mirror.

Rowe did not respond. She dropped her eyes and turned to sit back on her bed.

"What's wrong, Rowe? Have you been crying?"

Rowe turned away, gazing out the window. Keelie clearly saw that once again it hadn't been a good visit. She frowned.

"I guess it's a little tense around here, huh?"

"Tense?" Rowe sarcastically replied. "Where I come from, it's called acting. They're obviously pretending they're happy to see me, pretending they aren't ashamed of the dark spot in the family. Yes, Keelie, if that is what you call tense, then I would say it's been quite tense for the last 16 years."

"Oh, Rowe, that's not fair," Keelie softly replied, as she sat next to Rowe and stroked her hair. "I was here the night they took you away. Mom and Dad were devastated. It was very hard for them. It took Mom years to move on, and I'm not sure Dad ever got over it. They love you."

"Well, I'm sorry, Keelie!" Rowe retorted, "I can't tell, and I hate it here!"

"Rowe, you need to understand. It's not their fault. There is nothing anyone can do about it. It's the law. You have to visit, so at least try."

Rowe remained silent for a moment, contemplating whether she should say another word. As she looked into Keelie's eyes, she could see this clearly tore at her heart.

"Don't worry, Keelie, I can fix this—and one day I will," Rowe promised. I can change this whole thing. I can make sure Jenroe is gone and no one ever has to go through this again."

"*No*, Piper!" Keelie whispered in shock. She pulled away. "Don't ever say that again!"

Keelie suddenly sprang to her feet, rushing to the door to make sure no one was listening. Then she frantically searched Rowe's room.

"What are you doing?" Rowe asked.

"I'm looking for cameras! Piper, what you just said is dangerous. It's first-degree sedition, and it won't just get you sent to Exilium. Words like that could get you killed!" She gripped Rowe's shoulders and looked at her earnestly. "Promise me you will not say those things again!"

Rowe was surprised. Keelie had always encouraged her to be vocal, to speak her mind.

"I promise I won't speak that way again," Rowe softly replied. "But what about you, Keelie? Couldn't caring about me so much get you killed?"

Keelie suddenly paused. Her countenance hardened. "Jefferson would never allow that to happen, Piper! Don't think like that!"

"Are you sure?" Rowe looked at her cynically. "We all know that there are consequences for provoking the Jenroes."

She wished she hadn't said it. She could see the shock and hurt on Keelie's face.

"Piper, that's not fair! And what do you mean by consequences?"

"Well... I... I worry about you, and when my termination comes up, it might be best..."

"Don't even think of it!" Keelie snapped. "Would you really cut me out of your life?"

Rowe dropped her head, as she struggled to hold back her tears. She knew she could never cut Keelie out of her life. She loved her sister too much.

"No, Keelie," she finally replied, "of course not. I don't know how I could ever live without you. Forget I said that. I'm just scared and angry. I really do worry about you."

"Well, don't worry about me, Rowe," Keelie continued. "I'm going to be just fine, and so are you. Jefferson loves me, and I know that. He would never hurt me or allow anyone else to hurt me. So, erase those thoughts from your mind. Do we have a deal?"

"Yea," Rowe breathily replied. She turned to gaze out the window.

Keelie paused. Her heart broke to watch her little sister in so much pain.

"Well, I just wanted to come by and see you before Maya picked you up," she continued. "I had some business at the House of Missions and couldn't get here earlier. I promise I'll come see you in Righting if the Penses agree. Are you sure you're not hungry? I noticed you didn't finish your meal."

"No," replied Rowe. "You go ahead. I'll be okay."

Rowe collapsed on the bed and sighed. Only moments after Keelie left her room, there was another knock at her bedroom door. Rowe was sure it was Philmore or Patton letting her know that her mother had finally arrived.

"Come in."

To her surprise, as the door inched open, she found Jana waiting to be invited in. Rowe defiantly turned over, burying her face in her pillow. Jana was the last person she expected or wanted to see in the doorway. *Where is Mom?* She looked at her watch in frustration. For the first time in 16 years, Maya Pense was running late.

∞∞∞∞∞∞∞∞∞∞

Maya stood at a beautiful gravesite, only five miles from

the Sparrow home. She had stopped there, as she did each month, to place fresh flowers on the grave and to say a prayer. Unfortunately, on this visit, time had gotten away from her.

"I truly miss you," Maya sighed as she plucked a lone English Rose from the bouquet and placed it on the grave. "I will continue to give her all that you gave me, and one day I will make this all right for her. I promise. I will take care of her."

She looked down at her watch with a start. Rushing to the car, she called out behind her, "I have to go now. You know the rules. They're expecting me."

∞∞∞∞∞∞∞∞∞∞

Jana inched the door open further. "May I have a word with you?" she said softly as she entered Rowe's room.

Rowe shrugged nonchalantly. Even though she kept her gaze out the window, trying to focus only on the superbly manicured lawn, she couldn't ignore the loud smell of alcohol that accompanied Jana through the door. So much for whatever engagement this lady said she had.

"I know it must be hard coming here and always having to leave," Jana slurred, "but it was not my choice or your father's. We were forced to turn you over."

"You are such a drunken liar!" Rowe said coldly, tears consuming her face. "You signed those papers long before I was born, and I became no more than a blip in your memory once you were allowed to keep your precious Patton! But that's okay," she continued, wiping her face. Leaving here is not hard for me! That's where you are wrong! The hard part is coming here at all! I hate you. I hate Phil. I hate Patton!"

"We love you, Rowe…" Jana pleaded.

"Love me?" Rowe sarcastically questioned. "Oh, you had better not say that too loud. The Jenroes might disown you for loving a Sunz, but I'll say this… when you learn what real love is, then let me know. I would have died before I allowed anyone to take my child, no matter what she looked like. Maya Pense, my real mother, taught me about real love. The kind of love where you would die for your children— that's love, Jana! That's real love!"

Jana was a sobbing inebriated mess by the time Rowe finished, but she quickly regained her composure at the ring of the doorbell. Maya had returned.

"Get your things together," Jana said numbly as she stumbled towards the door.

It was strange to Rowe that Jana always met Maya outside. Initially, she believed that Jana didn't want her mother in the home, but often she found them having a cordial conversation. Once, when she was a very small child, she spied them hugging. Such affection was not normal for Jana. However, other than those short conversations while Rowe was being retrieved from her visits, Jana never mentioned Maya, nor did Maya mention Jana.

Rowe walked out while the Sparrows remained silent. Jana returned inside the home as Maya waited for Rowe in the car. They all knew it wouldn't be long before Rowe's monthly visits would become a thing of the past.

As Rowe and Maya pulled out of the driveway, Keelie returned inside the Sparrow home only to find her parents displaying an air of sadness.

"What did you say to her?" Keelie snapped at Jana and Philmore. "Why do you put her through this torture? She's happy with the Penses, so let her be. You think she wants to come here and be reminded that we live in a world that says she's not good enough to be a part of this family?"

"We have to follow the law, Keelie." Jana replied.

"Oh, Mom, don't give me that crap! You and Dad both know that Jeremy would give you a pass for Piper, so I can't understand why you would do this to her. She's only a child!"

"She's 16 years old, Keelie!" Philmore said.

"Yea, you know what, Dad? You're right, she's 16, and she'll be 17 in a couple of months, and 18 next year, and then you won't have the opportunity of getting some kind of sick enjoyment out of putting her through this!"

"You listen here, young lady," Philmore barked.

"No, Dad, *you* listen! I don't know what happened to you guys. You were genuinely hurt when they took Piper away. What happened?"

"She doesn't belong here, Keelie!" Patton yelled out. "Just accept it!"

Keelie spun around and faced him. "Oh, I do accept it, you little brat! I'm glad she doesn't have to be raised in this home and watch them spoil you rotten while you cut school, get high with your friends, and do everything but crack a book. You think you're better than Piper because your skin is lighter? Really? I actually visit with her, I actually spend time with her, and you know what? She's smarter than any of us. She's graduating high school soon, and she will already have her bachelor's degree. Don't you just wish, Patton, that you were half of what she is?"

The hurt in Patton's eyes was more than Keelie could take. She immediately regretted her words as he stormed out of the room.

"How dare you!" Jana interjected.

"How dare I?" Keelie sarcastically replied.

"Yes, Keelie, how dare *you*, Mrs. Jefferson Jenroe."

Jana grabbed her wine glass and flung it on the tile floor, shattering it to pieces, then pointed at Keelie. "The very people who took her out of here, the Jenroes—you chose to marry into that family. You are a part of the administration that originally made it illegal for Piper to live here. So, don't you come in here all high and mighty and tell us we're wrong. You are the one who will walk out that door and get in bed with the very ones who believe Piper is less than the rest of us. So, live with it."

Keelie was silent. She had been struggling for quite some time with her choice to marry Jefferson. Not long after they married, it became clear he strongly supported his father's policies, but she loved him with all her heart.

They had met during their freshman year of college in a

political science course. Jefferson attended college under the pseudonym of Dallas Craig, concealing his Jenroe identity. Keelie found herself in opposition to most if not all of the political arguments of the young Mr. Craig, who seemed quite amused with her political ideology and her utilitarian approach. Smitten with Keelie, Jefferson pursued her relentlessly until she finally agreed to a date. By the first date, she knew he was the one.

It was not until graduation that he finally revealed his true identity to her, but it was too late. She was very much in love with him. Keelie couldn't believe that after encouraging her to accept Jefferson's proposal, Jana was now ridiculing her for marrying him.

Just as the silence in the room became unbearable, Jana continued.

"I would have never signed papers agreeing to give up any of my children. I would have never thought…"

"Thought what, Mom?" said Keelie, now wiping her own tears. "You knew very well that none of us were pure. You knew there was a 50-percent chance that any of us could have been a Sunz, but you did it anyway. You aren't the one victimized. No matter how much this hurts, compared to Piper, you're not suffering, I'm not suffering, and neither are Dad or Patton. It's Piper who suffers the most, and the sad part is that she only suffers when she comes here to visit you! Just tell her, Mom! Tell her the entire truth!"

Chapter 6∞
THE JENROES

Keelie Jenroe struggled to see through the tears and torrential rain. She navigated heavier-than-usual traffic on her return to the House of Missions, formerly known as the White House. It was located in the center of Imperium, a short 10 miles from the Sparrow home, but tonight she would take a longer route. She needed time to think. As she plowed through the pounding rain, the last few years of her life flashed through her mind. The guilt of marrying Jefferson Jenroe, the successful son of President Jeremy Jenroe, tore through her heart. All she could feel was how she had abandoned Rowe. Nevertheless, the House of Missions was her home, and the Jenroe's were her family.

"Are you as extreme as your father?" she had asked Jefferson after learning his true identity years ago while they were dating.

"Are you really that attached to your Sunz sister?" Jefferson had retorted.

That had ended the conversation rather quickly. She never thought much more of the exchange as, honestly, she found him quite hard to resist. However, she continued to feel complete disdain for his father, Jeremy Jenroe, president of the United Missions of America. She dared not speak it though, not only for her safety but because she was very much smitten with his son. As she drove, her thoughts went back to one of the many times that Jefferson had shared his discomfort over her relationship with Rowe.

"Keelie, I know she's your biological sister, but she's a Sunz," he had warned. "Any attachment to her could tarnish your career options with the Droite Party, not to mention my own aspirations to succeed my father."

That very comment caused a break-up between them that lasted several months, prior to Jefferson's official proposal. She was grateful that Jana and Madeline, her mother-in-law, had been there for her and encouraged her to give him a second chance. Her biggest regret was that she had not held Jefferson to his vow.

He had promised that if she agreed to marry him, her love for Rowe was a topic that was off limits.

Keelie, I love you with all my heart. Those were the words that he had spoken so eloquently as he fell upon one knee in the presence of both of their families.

She only stared at him, waiting for the word, "yes" to come from her heart, but she stood there speechless in front of an entire ballroom of people. The silence lasted too long. She could see the humiliation that she was causing him, but she couldn't bring herself to say yes, because all she could think of was Rowe.

"I can't," she whispered through her tears as she stormed out of the ballroom.

However, as before, Jefferson was not willing to give up. As fast as she had run away from the crowded ballroom, he bolted directly behind her.

"Keelie," he sighed, "why won't you marry me?"

"I can't, Jefferson," she sobbed. "You said it yourself. My attachment to Rowe will always hinder us—hinder you. I love you with all my heart, but I'm not willing to abandon her. Not even for you."

"How about this, Keelie," he replied as he softly caressed her hand and returned to one knee. "The topic of your sister and your love for her is off limits. I will in no manner try to block or hinder your relationship if you agree to be my wife."

Keelie couldn't believe what she was hearing. He loved her so much that he was willing to go against the policies of his own father's administration just to have her in his life. She knew he loved her. How could she turn him away again?

"Yes," Keelie whispered through her tears.

"Did I hear you correctly?" Jefferson asked with a smile. "What did you say?"

Keelie loved Jefferson's smile. It always made her feel better, and the slight goofiness of it always made her laugh.

"Yes! Yes!" she gushed, laughing, as tears of sadness turned to tears of joy. "Yes, I will marry you!" Suddenly, she saw her mother standing at the entrance.

"She said yes!" Jana shouted back to all the guests in the ballroom. They erupted with cheer.

Not long after they were married, things slowly began to change. Eventually, Jefferson forbade her to discuss the topic of Rowe in the home, especially in the presence of his father.

"Keelie, my family is quite aware of your relationship with Rowe," he had said, "and although they do not approve, my father is very much appreciative of the loyalty and devotion that you have shown for the Droite Party. You were his best surrogate. So, all I ask is that you table the topic of your sister in the House of Missions, especially in the presence of my family."

Keelie's heart sank at his words. She loathed herself for defending the cruelty and hate of Jeremy Jenroe throughout his campaign, often outright denying his actions and the words he spoke, even though they could be proven. She secretly abhorred his policies but kept quiet.

"I compromised my principles to support many of your father's policies because of my love for you!" Keelie lashed. "How dare you go back on your promise to me? How dare you refer to my sister as a topic? She's a human being!"

"I understand that," said Jefferson, "but my family doesn't. If you love Rowe, I love Rowe. I promise you, Keelie, if and when I succeed my father, things will change, but until then, he is the president, and we must support him. Do you understand?"

"Yes, Jefferson," she submissively replied.

Although she loved Jefferson deeply, she hated feigning submissiveness. Her heart told her that beneath all the politics, he was really a good man, but her head told her that he was his father's son. She strongly questioned if he only told her what she wanted to hear. In many ways, Jefferson was nothing less than a kind and generous husband. However, as time passed, she sensed he despised her love for her Sunz sister. She was convinced, though, that he truly loved her for the bleeding-heart principles that she no longer felt comfortable sharing with him. She decided that in order to survive her marriage, she could no longer be fully honest with him.

"My love for my sister is just that, Jefferson," she had said as she cleared her throat. "I love her because she is my sister. I do not have those feelings for any other Sunz or Metisse other than the few Metisse in Imperium. Therefore, I do not object to any of your father's policies, and I will continue to support them."

Keelie knew she was not being honest with Jefferson. She deeply desired for the laws of the United Missions to change. The inequalities and the injustices were obvious and excessive.

How could her marriage last?

The ring of her cell phone startled her. The display on her

console told her it was Philmore.

"Hey, Dad, what's up?"

She attempted to hide the shakiness in her voice, that she had been crying since she had left his home.

"Hi, sweetie," said Philmore. "I was just calling to check on you. Your mother and I were concerned whether you'd made it back safely. This storm is pretty bad."

"I know," replied Keelie, "but don't worry, Dad. I'm not back yet only because I took a different route. I have a lot on my mind. I just needed to take a ride to clear my head."

There was deep silence on the other end. Keelie wondered if they had lost connection, but then, through the sound of pelting rain, she could make out his steady breathing.

"Dad is everything okay?"

"Keelie, I'm fine, but you are not. Now, I need you to listen to me. I know you love your sister, and when you are in our home, it's okay for you to express that. But, sweetie, you are playing a very dangerous game with the Jenroes."

"I know that, Dad! You don't think I know that?" Keelie retorted. "I am more worried about Jefferson finding out how much I truly hate this unjust regime. He wouldn't forgive me. I

M.J. Logan

can never let him know, at least not now."

"But, Keelie, why do you stay?"

Keelie's voice broke. "Dad, I stay because staying with Jefferson means having a better chance of protecting Rowe. I'm very confused. I may not be sure of much anymore, but one thing I am sure of is even though I love Jefferson, I love my sister more!"

Suddenly the signal dropped, and the call discontinued. The only sound was the steady beat of windshield wipers.

You are my only hope, Jefferson. She pulled into the private entrance of the House of Missions, turned off the car, and sat for a moment. *One day you will be president, then I can influence a change. Because I know you love me.*

∞∞∞∞∞∞∞∞∞∞∞

The House of Missions was quiet when she walked in. The secret service guard escorted her beyond the entrance of the home and gestured her toward the residence dining area.

"Ms. Keelie, Ms. Madeline requests that you join them in the residence dining hall," he informed. "The family is there preparing to dine for the evening."

"Thank you," Keelie replied as she headed down the long hall, not caring that her wet heels left marks on the plush carpet.

Madeline Jenroe, Jefferson's mother, whom she felt more endeared to than her own mother at times, greeted her with a warm hug and assisted her in removing her cloak.

"Good evening, Keelie," said Madeline, warmly. "I was wondering if you were going to join us for dinner this evening. How are Jana and the family?"

"Oh, they're fine, Madeline. Thanks for asking." A thick silence invaded the room as Keelie took her seat at the table beside her husband, Jefferson.

Jefferson leaned over and whispered, "I assume your visit was pleasing?"

"If you're asking if I was able to see Rowe, then yes," Keelie blurted.

Jefferson nervously shifted in his chair. His father, Jeremy Jenroe, immediately glowered at Keelie. The president's distrust for Keelie's loyalty was growing by the day. He'd warned Jefferson to get a handle on his wife before she became a problem.

"Unfortunately," Jeremy interjected, his hard glare locked on her, "those are the toils of this imperfect system that we must endure for now. Were it not for my beautiful wife, I would burn down the likes of all the other territories so as not to deal with those people. However, we must show some level of pity for them."

Keelie struggled to swallow the cool water from the dinner glass. She fought back the fiery flame of words she wished to spit out at Jeremy Jenroe. She knew that would be suicidal. Just across from her sat Patsy Hilleary, Jeremy Jenroe's blind sister. Although she could not see, she strongly sensed the animosity in Keelie's voice.

"You seem a bit preoccupied this evening, Keelie," said Patsy, coolly. "Did something happen on your visit that you care to share with the family?"

"Oh, let it go Patsy," said Madeline. "Keelie's obviously had an exhausting evening. I want her to maintain her strength. She and Jefferson are working on the first of the next generation of Jenroes, you know, and I for one am excited to someday soon become a grandmother." She smiled and winked at Keelie.

Jeremy Jenroe eyed his wife without saying a word.

"I'm not feeling very well," Keelie responded. "Please excuse me. Jefferson, I am going to retire for the evening. Take your time finishing your dinner."

As Keelie left the residence dining, Jeremy Jenroe called

out to her.

"Keelie, by the way, speaking of our future grandchildren, have you signed the biological law documentation? You know it's imperative that you sign that before any child is born."

Keelie took a deep breath and fixed her countenance. She forced a smile before turning to face her father-in-law. "Unfortunately, I am not with child yet. However, we are trying, therefore, once we are given the good news, I will gladly cooperate with the biological law."

Keelie hastily exited the residence dining hall.

Once she was sure Keelie was far from the dining hall, Madeline Jenroe angrily turned to her husband.

"Oh, Jeremy, I'm appalled. How could you say that to Keelie? She's been very loyal to you and this family. She's an asset to your administration, if I must say. Don't scare the poor child off."

"It's not my intent to scare her off," President Jenroe aloofly responded. "However, you..." he jabbed his finger in the air in the direction of his son, "...*you* need to get a handle on that young lady. Jackson had the same problem. Did you not, Jackson?"

Jackson Jenroe, the brother of the president, sat to the right of his blind sister, Patsy Hilleary and coldly stared at Jefferson.

"My wife, God rest her soul," Jackson condescendingly spoke, "was cursed with the same bleeding heart for those Sunz people in Righting…"

"She does *not* have empathy for the Sunz as a people!" Jefferson countered. "…only her biological sister. Keelie fully supports this administration and believes her sister is in a good home in Righting."

He pushed back his plate and abruptly stood. "The topic at this dinner table will not be my wife, and I will not sit here for another minute of this." He stormed out of the residence dining hall.

Patsy broke the silence that followed. Even though she was blind, it seemed her cold, blank stare could penetrate to the soul. "Jeremy, the future of our family's power lies in your boy's hands. You cannot allow that young woman to influence him. It will change the Droite Party forever." "Oh, Patsy, leave them alone," said Madeline, nervously.

"They're young now, and Keelie has shown us nothing but

loyalty."

"Are you sure about that?" her husband interjected. Madeline paused and looked down.

"Not to worry, Patsy," Jeremy continued with no emotion. My son is *fully* dedicated to the administration. Should that wife of his get out of hand, there are ways of dealing with her."

"Well, I think that deserves a toast," Patsy replied in a raspy voice. She raised her wine glass to her lips, donning her signature sinister smirk.

∞∞∞∞∞∞∞∞∞

As Keelie Jenroe prepared for the night, she stood in the mirror and examined herself. Checking her reflection from all angles, she imagined what she would look like with child. She could hear the creak of the bedroom door as Jefferson entered. Finally, he had come to join her.

"Keelie, are you in there?" he called out as he stood outside the bathroom door.

"Be out in a minute," Keelie replied.

However, he was through the door before she could finish her words. Jefferson Jenroe loved Keelie with all his heart. He could clearly see that something was bothering her. He suspected what it was but dreaded it, so he refused to acknowledge the truth. Her beauty astounded him as he embraced her from behind. He slowly caressed her shoulders as his lips brushed across the delicate porcelain skin of her neck.

"You get more beautiful every time I see you," he said.

Keelie smiled at the reflection of the two of them in the mirror.

"I'm going to get a shower," said Jefferson, as he began to disrobe.

"That's fine," said Keelie, as she walked into the bedroom. "I'll be waiting."

Keelie felt ashamed. She continued to keep a secret from her husband that could surely destroy them. It wasn't until she was sure the shower was running that she pulled the small package of pills out of the miniature clutch. She always kept them well hidden in her bag. Quickly swallowing the pills, she relaxed on the large canopy bed and stared at the enormous oval ceiling. If Jefferson were to find out she would lose him forever, but she knew in her heart that she would never sign over a child of hers to be taken away— and the pills would assure that she would never have to.

Keelie looked up to see Jefferson with only a towel wrapped around his waist. She loved her husband. He was more handsome to her each time she encountered him. As she sat up in the bed, Jefferson joined her, softly touching the silk gown that she had been given as a wedding gift.

"You are absolutely amazing," he whispered. He slowly kissed her and dimmed the lights.

Chapter 7∞
The Mark—One Year Later

Rowe was only two months from her 18th birthday. Graduation had come and gone, and she had earned both her high school diploma and her degree in advanced technology. Alfred and Maya had agreed with her decision to take a term off to spend time with them before leaving for graduate school. Her birthday celebration would be held at Righting Court, the political house for the Righting territory. This was a smaller version of the House of Missions. It was where territory leaders and administrative officers met to conduct political business as part of the Politico Mission. Fortunately, due to his rank as brigadier general, Alfred was able to reserve the state dining hall for Rowe's celebration.

"So, how many guests are we talking about here?" Maya

asked excitedly, pen in hand. She sat down across from Rowe at the kitchen table.

Rowe gave a half shrug. "I don't know. I know you and Dad want to invite people, but can we please keep it small?"

"Are you sure about that?" asked Maya, fairly disappointed but knowing Rowe didn't have many friends.

"Well, I want to pay for this myself, if you and Dad don't mind. I need to learn to be more independent. That's why I took the job at *Right Word*."

Rowe was proud of herself. She had decided to take on a small job in the mail room of the local paper and was saving all of her earnings. She was practicing money management for when she relocated to the east side of the territory to attend graduate school. She reasoned it was important for her mom and dad to support her new independent stance.

"How about your new friends from the paper?" Maya suggested.

"What friends?" Rowe asked as she aloofly scribbled on the list.

"I really don't consider the other kids at the paper my friends. Even though most of them are older than me, they're immature."

She hesitated. "But you can put Harper on the list."

"Your boss?" Maya raised her eyebrows.

"Yeah, he's really cool. He thinks . . . I should go for junior reporter," said Rowe, pretending to look over her list to avoid eye contact.

Maya shifted nervously in her chair.

"I don't think that's such a good idea, Rowe. Remember, no jobs that require . . ."

"I know, Mom!" Rowe shot back. "You've been warning me for as long as I can remember. That's exactly why I told Harper I wasn't interested right now . . . but the truth is, I am, and you and Dad just have to trust me!"

The room was silent. Maya put down her pen and leaned back in her chair. She sensed something had changed in her daughter since that last visit with the Sparrows. Since then, tensions had been high at home. Adding fuel to the fire, Rowe was not happy that the Sparrows were on the guest list. The only member of her biological family that she wanted to attend the celebration was Keelie.

Rowe looked at her mother and softened.

"I'm sorry for yelling, Mom. But you and Dad need to know the truth. I do still write, but I can control it now. The stories only manifest now if I allow them to."

Maya tensed. "How...?"

"With practice, Mom. At first it was difficult, but I never wrote stories that could hurt us. I can now control the endings. I just have to follow the story. I promise I have no plans to use it. I am fully aware of the dangers, but I'm almost an adult now."

Rowe slipped into the chair next to Maya and put her arm around her mother's shoulders.

"You should know you can trust me, Mom. I wouldn't do anything to jeopardize our safety, especially with Dad being in the position he's in. Don't you think I understand that my actions impact all of our lives? Anyway, I'm concentrating on my next black belt level right now. I told Harper that I would consider it, but sixth-degree black belt comes first."

Maya's shoulders slumped. She was at a loss for words. Rowe took her pause as an opportune time to leave for practice. Maybe all she had shared just needed time to sink in.

"Speaking of black belt," said Rowe, turning on the faucet to fill her water bottle, "I'm headed to the gym for a while. I'll be back in time for dinner."

"Not so fast, young lady," said Maya. "Your Dad and I worry about you. We're not trying to control you, but you could place yourself in a great deal of danger if anyone discovers you have that gift."

"Well, no one will," Rowe retorted, "and as I've said before, you are just going to have to trust me."

"I do trust you!" Maya snapped, "but I worry about your relationship with the Sparrows."

"Really?" Rowe gave a bitter laugh. "Are you afraid that I would do something to them? Oh, Mom, I wouldn't even waste my energy!"

"Piper Sparrow!" Maya roses from her seat. "What have I always taught you? You have to learn to let go of all the hurt! You have to forgive the Sparrows. Your situation was out of their control...."

"Okay, Mom...yea, yea, yea." Rowe snapped shut the lid on her water bottle and spun around.

"Forgiveness, forgiveness, I get it. It wasn't their fault, and I just need to forgive them. Enough said, because I don't want to get into another conversation about how forgiveness is going to save my soul."

Maya drew a long breath and closed her eyes. Rowe's stubbornness was impenetrable. *Dear God, help her. Help me.*

Maya held out her arms. Rowe walked into them, giving her mom a reluctant hug.

"Well, I'll let it go for today," Maya said, lovingly tucking a lock of Rowe's hair behind her ear. "But one day you will realize that forgiveness is the only way, Rowe. Your ability to forgive the Sparrows is not for their sake. It's for your own peace of mind."

"I understand, Mom." There was a long pause. "I'm going to head to the gym now."

She planted a kiss on Maya's cheek.

"No work today?" Maya asked.

"No, not today. See you in a bit."

Rowe grabbed her gym bag and headed out the door.

∞∞∞∞∞∞∞∞∞

The heavy stench of sweat filled the crowded gym. Winnie grabbed a towel, wiped the sweat from her forehead, and told Rowe to take a water break. In actuality, she needed the break herself. Rowe was more skilled and more relentless than ever. As her sparring partner and trainer, Winnie was glad of Rowe's progress, but it was becoming harder and harder to find ways to challenge her. She needed to be especially hard on her today, because her sixth-degree belt would be by far the most difficult to attain. Rowe had exceeded the skill levels of even Brigadier General Pense's most well-trained militia men.

Winnie realized that Rowe was quickly surpassing her own skills. Sparring with her had become quite difficult, but Winnie remained loyal to the general and agreed to continue to train his daughter. General Pense had increased her rank in the Mission and had helped to get her family out of poverty. The few bumps and bruises she received training Rowe was nothing compared to the starvation she had suffered as a child.

There was something else Winnie stood to gain. She was very much aware that sparring with her prized student was making her own skills better—ones she would soon use for something far greater than competition. But there was more. Winnie tilted her head as she watched Rowe return from her break. She drew a deep breath. Yes, training Rowe was only the tip of the iceberg.

∞∞∞∞∞∞∞∞∞∞

Rowe felt as if she were on fire. All the energy and frustration from the past month—her visit with the Sparrows, the stress of exams, planning her graduation, tension with her parents, transitioning to independence—had built to a crescendo as she spun and kicked, swiftly battling through a mirage of strikes and counter strikes. She was completely absorbed in her maneuvers, so it took a moment for her to notice him.

The stranger stood in the far corner of the gym. He stared at her, intently eyeing her every move. At first, Rowe dismissed it. It wasn't long, however, before the stranger's glare penetrated her concentration, and the next thing she saw was stars. She found herself pinned to the gym floor with the pain of Winnie's take-down surging through her body.

"Ouch!" Rowe yelled, massaging the back of her neck. "That was harsh!"

"You're distracted," said Winnie, as she stood and held out her hand to pull her up. "What's going on?"

Rowe remained silent. Winnie followed her glance to the stranger. His glare remained locked on Rowe as he slowly rose to his feet and gestured toward the black wrist band on his arm. Purposefully, he removed it and revealed his wrist to her. Slowly, he placed the hood of his jacket over his head and swiftly exited the gymnasium.

"Follow him!" Winnie demanded in a whisper. "Follow him now!"

Rowe was surprised at her command.

"What?"

"Go, follow him now!" Winnie demanded.

Rowe paused. Her heart pounded. There was no time to think. Against her instincts, she darted out of the gym and quickly ran after the stranger.

"Hey . . . hey . . . Mr. . . . Sir!" she called out. The closer Rowe got to him, the faster the stranger walked. As Rowe closed in, he began to jog, then broke into an all-out run. Rowe tried to catch up, rounding the corner of the building where she had seen him vanish, but he was nowhere in sight.

Rowe was in awe of what the stranger had revealed to her under the wrist band. He had the exact same birthmark on his wrist as she had on her inner thigh. Her thoughts whirled. *Who was he? How was Winnie connected to this stranger?*

∞∞∞∞∞∞∞∞∞∞

Rowe lay on the floor of her room and bounced a small ball off the wall. She couldn't get the strange encounter at the gym out of her head. Question after question ran through her mind.

Why does this man have the same birthmark as me? Why was he trying to hide it? What did Winnie know about this man?

Suddenly, a few things became clear. Maya and Alfred had always forbidden her to wear shorts, other than ones just above her knees. She never had a problem with it, but now she was sure it was to hide the mark.

∞∞∞∞∞∞∞∞∞∞

The sound of the rising garage door told Rowe that her father had arrived.

It also alerted Maya.

"Your dad's home," Maya called out from the kitchen. "Get ready for dinner."

There was no response. Maya glanced towards Rowe's bedroom door and wrinkled her brow.

"Smells good in here," Alfred said as he entered the kitchen. "Where's Rowe? I'm starving."

"She's in her room. I called her just a moment ago, but she didn't answer. I don't know what's going on . . ."

"Well, join the club!" Rowe quipped, standing in the doorway, hand on her hip, with only her undergarments on."

"Young lady!" Alfred gasped as he turned away from his daughter. "That is quite inappropriate! Go clothe yourself immediately."

"No!" Rowe yelled in defiance. "Not until both of you tell me what this means!" She pointed at the mark just inside of her inner thigh. Alfred and Maya traded glances and lowered their heads.

"Tell me!" Rowe demanded. "What does this mean?"

"Rowe," Alfred said with a deep sigh, "go to your room and put on some clothes, and I will tell you, but not until you dress yourself, young lady."

Rowe balled her fists in defiance and went back inside her room, slamming the door behind her.

Moments later, she re-entered the kitchen and sat down to dinner. The clanging of forks magnified the silence. Rowe only moved her food around on her plate.

"Eat your dinner, young lady," Alfred said. "Just because you're almost 18 doesn't mean you can do as you wish around here!"

"I want to know what the mark means, if you know, Dad. Why won't you tell me?"

Alfred drew in a long breath and looked at Maya. She nodded, so he began. He shared with Rowe all that he knew about the mark. When he had finished, he asked the question that burned inside of him.

"How did you find out that the mark had a meaning?"

"I saw a man today," Rowe replied. "He was watching me as I sparred with Winnie. I saw his mark on his wrist. Based on what you just told me, he's just like me."

Alfred's heart pounded. "Are you sure it was the same mark?"

"Yes, I'm sure," Rowe replied. "It was on his wrist. He wanted me to see it."

Maya looked at Alfred nervously.

"I forbid you to return to that gym!" demanded Alfred, pounding his fist on the table. "He evidently knows who you are, and he could be dangerous. I'll find another place for Winnie to work with you."

"Well, you don't have to worry about that," Rowe replied under her breath.

"What was that?" demanded Alfred.

Rowe wished she had kept quiet. "Winnie was the one

who told me to follow him!"

"Winnie?" Alfred was in shock.

"Yes, Winnie! I ran after him but couldn't catch up. When I went back to the gym, Winnie was gone. All she left me was this note."

She reached in her pocket and pulled out a torn piece of paper. Alfred snatched it, and read the scribbled message:

You are ready.

He stared at it as if it had been a long message, then crumpled it up. His voice was controlled, yet stern. "I forbid you to return to that gym. And as for Winnie, . . . I will handle that." He abruptly rose and took his plate to the sink. Rowe glowered at him.

Alfred pivoted and walked back, standing in front of her. His presence was imposing. "Don't give me that look. You will not go back. I'm only doing what's in your best interest."

Maya's side glances warned Rowe to respond respectfully, but she was far from feeling compliant.

"You know what? Fine, Dad. Everything is in my best interest! What about what I want? What about what I need to know and understand?"

"You know enough!" Maya broke in. "Honestly, I feel the sooner you're off to graduate school, the better."

". . . And what if I've changed my mind?" Rowe stormed. "What if I want to stay at the *Right Word* and put off grad school a little longer? I'm still young enough to do it."

"Don't even think of it!" said Maya. "You will go to grad school. We won't hear another word of this nonsense."

Alfred regained his composure. "I will make the arrangements for your sixth-degree challenge tomorrow at a different gym. Now, eat your dinner. You will need your energy."

Rowe sat silently, feeling defeated. The interface with her parents had only served to fuel her curiosity about the stranger. She had a deep sense there was more. What were they hiding from her? What did her mother mean by, "You know enough?" How much more was there to know? Why did she sense they were in such a rush to get rid of her?"

Chapter 8∞
The Uninvited Guest

Righting Court buzzed with the most distinguished citizens of Righting Territory for Rowe's 18th birthday celebration. As the crowd began to mingle in the beautifully adorned ballroom, Rowe felt as if for one moment she might actually be in Imperium. Righting Court Ballroom was an expansive room of elegantly cascading crystal chandeliers, white columns, and beautifully decorated tables for the guests.

So much for the small guest list, Rowe thought, chuckling to herself. She watched Keelie and Maya busily scurrying through the growing crowd. She was proud to see her mom and sister working together and knew that it was because they both loved her. She smiled as she watched them graciously greet guests and make sure that the serving staff provided everyone with pre-meal hors d'oeuvres and light refreshments. In the midst of the gathering mass, she caught her mom's eye. Maya flashed a smile, winked, and headed toward her. Rowe sensed she was especially pleased to see a smile on her face. Her mother had not had that pleasure for quite some time. The past few weeks had been filled with tension in the Pense household. But tonight, seeing her mother's reaction to her in the beautiful blue gown that perfectly matched her eyes set a positive mood for Rowe.

"You look absolutely stunning!" said Maya.

"Thanks, Mom. You did a great job on this gown."

Maya's smile faded. "Oh, it looks like Jana and Philmore have arrived, and they look quite uncomfortable. Go greet them Rowe and be nice."

"Do I have to?" Rowe whispered.

"Yes, you do! Now, they have come out to help you celebrate this day, and you will be courteous. Besides, they love you regardless of what you believe, and someday you will realize that. How could they not love such a beautiful daughter? Now, go on."

Rowe stood there for a moment. She stared at Jana and Philmore, contemplating how to receive them as she stuffed her emotions deep inside. She completely missed how the rest of the guests stared at her in awe. She was absolutely stunning—exotic and beautiful. The rarity of her blue eyes with her caramel-colored skin gave her a glow that outshined everyone at the event. It was clearly her day, and she was very proud of herself for all that she had accomplished.

"Rowe go over and greet the Sparrows," Maya urged again, snapping her out of her trance. "It's common courtesy."

Rowe glared at the Sparrows. She noticed they were engaged in exchanging cordialities with her boss, Harper Whitson. She sighed. At least Harper's presence would make it easier for her to comply.

"Sure, Mom." She flashed a fake smile and headed in their direction.

"Well, my goodness, you look absolutely stunning!" Harper exclaimed as he greeted Rowe with a kiss on the cheek.

"You clean up well yourself," Rowe replied, smiling. She turned her attention to the Sparrows. "Jana, Philmore, Patton," Rowe acknowledged with a nod. "Thanks for coming."

"Oh, we wouldn't dream of missing this," Philmore gushed, turning to Jana for agreement. "Would we?"

Jana was already engrossed in her second glass of wine and

quite inebriated, considering the event had just begun.

"Oh . . . yes . . ." Jana finally answered after a long pause.

Harper cleared his throat, noticing the subtle tension between Rowe and her biological family.

"Well, I can clearly see where those exotic eyes come from, Rowe," Harper complimented. "Your mothers are striking, and you and your twin brother are exceptionally similar."

"Well, that's very nice of you, Harper," Rowe flatly replied before the rest of what she really wanted to say tumbled out. "You're right, Jana is stunning, but she's not my mother. Maya Pense is my mother. Jana was only a surrogate. Wouldn't you agree, Jana?"

Harper looked down and picked a piece of lint from his sleeve. A countenance of embarrassment crept over Jana's face, and the pain in her eyes was very real. She reached for her third glass of wine as one of the servers brushed by. Rowe went in for the kill.

"Secondly, please be aware that Patton doesn't like it when people say we look alike. Do you, Patton? Now if you will excuse me, my family is ready to begin."

Rowe turned with an air of satisfaction and walked toward

Alfred and Maya, dismissively calling out over her shoulder, "I hope you enjoy yourselves, and thanks again for coming out."

Keelie excitedly grabbed Rowe's hand, pulling her through the crowd. "It's time to begin! Your parents are ready."

As Rowe stood under the bright gleaming lights of the ballroom, all of the guests chattered about her stunning beauty.

"May I have your attention?" Alfred Pense announced. "I thank each of you for attending this special celebration. Maya and I, along with Piper's biological family, the Sparrows, are very proud of this young lady. As you all know, we refer to her as Rowe. Not only is she 18 years old today, but last spring, she completed her high school diploma, as well as a bachelor's degree in advanced scientific technology. Further, we proudly announce that she has been accepted to graduate school in the eastern part of Righting. Sadly, she will depart our home next term."

The guests gave Rowe a standing ovation. Rowe glanced over the crowd and her gaze stopped on Patton. He was flushed and ill at ease.

"However," Alfred continued, "as both her father and a brigadier general in the United Missions militia, I am proud to present this awesome young lady with her sixth-degree black belt in the militia defense program."

As the guests cheered wildly, Rowe watched as Patton stormed out of the ballroom with Philmore attempting to stop him.

Rowe exited the stage and Keelie met her, pulling her into an embrace. "I'm so proud of you,"she said. She noticed the stillness in Rowe's demeanor. "What's up, sis?"

Rowe drew in a long breath, then she pulled her away from the crowd. "I opted for termination of the biological law. I'm choosing cessation of my relationship with the Sparrows." Rowe struggled to look at Keelie. Her sister's eyes brimmed with tears.

"I understand, Piper. I knew this day would come. It's your choice."

Rowe grabbed Keelie's hands and looked at her warmly. "Don't cry. I didn't add your name to the list. I want you to remain a part of my life, Keelie. That's if you want to."

"Of course, I do!" She gave her a reassuring hug. "Well, you'd better get back to the guests. We can hang out later."

As Rowe worked her way back into the crowd, Keelie grabbed a cup of punch and headed over to join Jana, more to steady her mother than for the small talk. Seven glasses of wine in two hours had taken their toll on Jana, but Keelie would not let it ruin her night. She was consumed with the relief of knowing that Piper was not terminating their relationship. As she lifted the cup of punch to her lips she nearly choked with shock. Jefferson Jenroe entered the ballroom. The Sparrows looked on in surprise.

"Well, he must really love you," Jana said with a smirk.

"Why would he be here?" Keelie whispered.

She quickly walked over to him. "Honey, what brings you here?"

"I am here to deliver the termination papers," Jefferson announced vociferously, more to the crowd than to answer her question. "She's 18 today, and this has to be carried out."

"I *know* how old she is today, Jefferson," Keelie hissed.

"She's my biological sister. Why are you doing this?"

"She chose termination, and that includes you, too, Keelie."

He grabbed her by the arm and pointed her towards the door.

"You should head home now. I'll be home soon. I want to make sure this is done right, and given the circumstances, Keelie, this is an embarrassment having you in Righting. You don't belong here. You belong in Imperium, and frankly, I don't want my future children knowing they have a Sunz for an aunt."

"*What* children?" Keelie asked, incredulously. She yanked her arm out of his grasp. "We don't have any children, now do we? And if you do this, Jefferson Jenroe, we never will. Rowe would never put me on that list. She promised me that my name wasn't on it."

"Well, I'm sorry, Keelie, but she did." Jefferson forcefully placed the papers in Keelie's hand. "Maybe she was afraid to tell you. I think it's best if you don't confront her about it today. I mean, you wouldn't want to ruin her event, now would you?"

Keelie scanned the termination papers in shock. The words blurred through her tears. She slowly gazed across the room until her eyes met her sister's. Piper smiled at her. Suddenly Keelie's mind flashed back to her biological visit the previous year.

"*. . . There are consequences for lying down with the Jenroes!*" she remembered Piper warning.

"But she promised!" Keelie whispered, her chest rising and falling in rapid breaths.

"I know," Jefferson went on, "but she lied. She's a Sunz, Keelie. She can't be trusted. She never meant it when she said she was worried about how you would take this. And how dare she question my love and loyalty to you!"

"Wh . . . what do you mean?" Keelie sputtered. "How . . . *how* would you know that?"

"W . . . well . . . she said it to me at the preparation of the papers," Jefferson mumbled, clearing his throat. "She wanted to make sure you would be okay if she put your name on the papers. Honestly, I was aghast that she would turn on you in such a manner and then have the audacity to invite you here today."

Keelie's mind reeled. She found herself questioning every word coming out of her husband's mouth. She couldn't believe that Rowe would speak so openly with Jefferson about their relationship. But she couldn't let on that she didn't trust him. Was the Jenroe administration surveilling her? If not, how did he know so many details of a conversation that she had with her sister over a year ago? She wanted to run to Piper and warn her to read the papers fully before signing them, but she didn't want Jefferson to know she was suspicious. There had to be some other explanation. Thoughts swam around her.

Jefferson wouldn't dare betray me, would he? But she knew in her heart that Rowe wouldn't either.

"She looks happy," Keelie softly whispered.

"Yes, she does," Jefferson agreed, satisfied. "And now, we can all be happy. On second thought, I'll allow you to stay, but I want you home in an hour."

Suddenly, General Pense approached.

"Welcome to Righting, Mr. Jenroe," Alfred said. He extended his hand cordially.

Jefferson eyed Alfred in disgust, refusing his sincere gesture.

"Mr. Pense, I have only come to attain your daughter's signature for confirmation of termination."

"Oh, sure," Alfred responded slowly, gesturing for Rowe to join them.

A soft silence fell across the ballroom as the pen was placed in Rowe's hand. With a strong grip on it, she took a circumferential gaze around the room. Surprisingly, she had no second thoughts about biological termination as her gaze passed over Jana and Philmore, standing by anxiously. The smirk of satisfaction Patton donned as he slowly re-entered the room and realized what was transpiring was enough to push Rowe into gladly signing. Before she knew it, her signature stared back at her.

She handed the signed document over to Jefferson and glanced one last time at Jana Sparrow, stumbling away in a drunken stupor. Rowe watched in disgust, and relief slowly began to wash over her. She knew she had made the right choice.

But there was plenty Rowe did not know. She did not know that her biological mother stumbled away because her heart had dropped into her stomach. She did not know that Jana had not felt this level of pain and loss since that night many years ago when the medical mission had taken her daughter away. She did not know that her mother had convinced herself that she had survived well beyond those feelings—and that if ever she did struggle, alcohol would numb it. She also did not know that at that very moment, her mother realized how very wrong she had been.

As Jana teetered into the powder room, Rowe scanned the room for Keelie. Their eyes locked, and Rowe flashed her a smile. It quickly faded. Keelie showed no signs of emotion but turned and walked away.

Across the room, as Rowe stared after her, Keelie knew she had to leave. She was baffled. She was hurt. Why was Rowe smiling at her? She couldn't bear the pain anymore and turned away. She had to get outside.

Why would Piper smile at me if she knows she's cutting me out of her life? Something's not right.

But hadn't she seen her name on those papers? Hadn't she watched Piper sign them and Jefferson retrieve them from her possession as he quickly folded them over and secured them inside his suit jacket? Her emotions swarmed around her.

She headed out the same doors her husband had walked through moments earlier, but before she could collect her thoughts, Philmore joined her. She sensed that his pain rivaled her own.

"Well, Keelie, I guess there's nothing left here for your mother and I to do. We're heading home."

He knew his tone did little to hide his own loss, deep internal struggle, and confusion. He didn't know whether to be infuriated, devastated, or simply happy for Piper. He thought back to earlier in the evening as he had watched his daughter standing at the front of ballroom. Why did Alfred have the right to take his place?

Wasn't it my genetics that made her so beautiful? Wasn't

it my genetics that made her so smart and talented? Why do I have to stand by idle, as if I'm a complete stranger?

He tried to shake off his feelings and put his arm around Keelie. At least he could focus on the one daughter he did have. Just accept things the way they are, he told himself. But his heart pounded in his chest. It told him Piper would always be a part of it. He would never forgive himself for allowing the medical mission to take her away. He would always blame himself for allowing his wife to fall from a woman of grace into a haphazard drunk, unable to love and care for the family she had remaining. However, one thing consoled him. Being with Alfred and Maya was the best place that Piper could be. With them, she was closer to him and Jana than she actually knew. Maybe someday she would find out . . . maybe someday.

Patton joined them.

"Where did your mother run off to?"

"She went to the ladies' room," Patton replied nonchalantly.

"Well, she's taking awfully long. I think it's time we leave. Its clear Piper wants nothing more to do with us, so we'd better get back to Imperium."

"I'll go check on Mom," Keelie said.

"Please, let the Penses know that we'll be leaving," Philmore said.

As Keelie entered the powder room, she heard the soft whimper of her mother. She silently walked over to where Jana Sparrow sat alone, slumped on the floor. Keelie knelt down and embraced her.

"It's okay, Mom. If it makes you feel any better, my name was on the termination list, too."

Jana turned to Keelie in shock. "That can't be right. Piper would never do that."

"Well, she did, Mom. I saw it for myself. We just have to hope that she'll be fine. She's probably upset that I married Jefferson. I don't much blame her. It's probably best for her if we just let her live her life. At this point, all we can do is be happy for her. I'm sure Piper will have a wonderful life. She's an amazing young lady."

Jana's tears continued to flow. She slowly stood in front of the mirror and composed herself as Keelie gently consoled her.

"Here, take these," Keelie said, handing her a tissue. Jana had a look of panic in her eyes.

I never wanted to let her go, Keelie. You do know that, don't you?"

Keelie turned away from her mother in silence. She didn't know what to believe anymore. She was still questioning the termination papers, not knowing whether Rowe or Jefferson had betrayed her. As they exited the powder room and headed outside, Patton and Philmore, along with Rowe and the Penses, were waiting.

Rowe was relieved to see Keelie. She had not been able to look the rest of her biological family in the eyes. But as she smiled at Keelie, she noticed her distress.

"You take care of our little girl, Alfred," said Philmore, as he turned to walk down the stairs of Righting Court. Keelie and the rest of his family followed.

"They seem very sad," said Maya, as they walked back inside the ballroom. "Are you sure you made the right decision?"

"Yes, I'm sure!" said Rowe. "I don't care if I ever see the three of them again."

"Three?" asked Maya, furrowing her eyebrows. "You do realize that Keelie's name was on the list as well?"

Panic gripped Rowe.

"But . . . but I specifically said that I didn't want Keelie's name on that list! I wrote the names in myself, and Keelie was not included."

Maya was silent.

Rowe's body shook. She darted back toward the grand double doors of Righting Court and threw them open. As she reached the towering steps of the building, she barely caught a glimpse of the limousine carrying Keelie as it rounded the corner with the Sparrows not far behind.

"Keelie!" she screamed. "Keelie . . . Keelie . . . Please don't go!"

But her words were lost in the night air. She slumped down on the towering steps and hugged herself. *Why hadn't Keelie said something? How could this happen?*

She shivered as a breeze whipped at her tresses. She was alone and confused. Of course, she would always have Alfred and Maya, but Keelie—her only connection to her true identity—was gone. She buried her face in her beautiful blue dress and sobbed until it was wet.

Only moments passed, but to Rowe, it felt as if she had been sitting on the steps of Righting Court for hours. As she pulled herself up, something startled her. A soft hint of a hand touched her shoulder. She expected to see her dad, but she drew a sharp breath. Through a bit of moonlight that filtered through the branches, she recognized him—the stranger. Even in the shadows, with his face hidden beneath his hoodie, she knew it was the man from the gym. He gave her a small card and swiftly turned to walk away. She looked down at it.

DiCaprio~ You will know how to find me when the time is right.

Chapter 9∞
The Switch

The unfortunate events at the end of the party left Rowe in a sullen mood. Held up in her room for hours, refusing to come out except for dinner, she attempted several times to make contact with Keelie, but all numbers of her former family had been blocked. Panicked and depressed, Rowe had no idea what to do. She was sure this was Jefferson Jenroe's doings. He must have covertly added Keelie's name to the list.

As Rowe sat on the edge of her bed, the card from the stranger caught her eye. She picked it up and dismissively turned it over and over. She had been so consumed with missing Keelie that the second encounter with the stranger had taken a back seat. She found the clandestine encounter with him not only eerie, but exasperating. If he was interested in her because of the mark, why didn't he just say so?

"I will get my sister back in my life," she whispered as she stared at the card. "Then I will find you, DiCaprio." She tossed the card back on her nightstand.

Rowe had to figure out who was responsible for adding her sister's name to the termination papers. Only a day had passed since the party, yet an air of gloom had settled on the Pense home. Alfred and Maya did everything in their power to cheer their daughter up, but to no avail. Highly concerned for her, Maya informed Alfred that she was sure Jefferson Jenroe was responsible for adding Keelie's name to the termination list.

"The good news, Maya, is that Rowe will be leaving for school in a few months," Alfred had consoled her. "Once she gets there, she will meet new people and make new friends. It won't be long before she puts this all behind her."

Alfred seemed so sure of himself, but feelings of uncertainty plagued Maya's heart. She watched her despondent daughter, who was barely able to finish her dinner, continue to struggle with the loss of her sister.

"Mom, I'm going to bed," Rowe mumbled. She excused herself from the dinner table and headed to her room.

This night was pivotal for Rowe, and unfortunately, Maya

and Alfred Pense were not privy to it. As Rowe's emotions intensified, so did her desperation and hunger for revenge. She made up her mind that she was not going to allow the Jenroes to deprive her any further. She was done with their tactics, and she was determined to have her sister back in her life.

Rowe closed her bedroom door. She grabbed her tablet from the bedside table, and turned off her lamp, while setting herself up under her covers with a clip-on reading light and cautiously taking care that neither Alfred nor Maya would suspect she was still awake. She furiously began to write. As she continued to write, she could hear them heading to their room to retire for the evening. Just as the house was completely quiet, she wrote the last word. She threw off the covers and swung her feet over the bed. A bright light appeared in the closet, just across the room. Rowe stood and slowly approached it, opened the door, and entered the portal.

∞∞∞∞∞∞∞∞∞∞∞

As morning crept into the House of Missions, Keelie Jenroe prepared for her day. She had awakened with a heavy heart. Despite the events that had transpired, she told herself that what was most important was what was best for Piper. As she scooped up a lump of laundry from the bedroom floor, the termination papers fell from the pocket of Jefferson's suitcoat that he had worn to Righting Court. Unable to resist, Keelie quickly opened them. She gasped. Just as Piper had said, her name was not listed. But hadn't she seen it there herself? She spun around and ran down the hallway to meet Jefferson who was coming up the stairs.

"Jefferson! Look! Did you know this? I could have sworn that my name was on these termination papers the other night."

In a panic, Jefferson darted up the rest of the steps two at a time and furiously snatched the papers from Keelie.

"What is this? Your name was here! I . . . I . . ."

"You did what? Jefferson? What did you do?"

"Well, I saw it too," he said.

"Well, it's not there now. I'm going to see my sister to clear this up." Keelie hurried into the study and made a copy of the termination papers. Then she angrily tossed the originals toward Jefferson and grabbed her coat and keys.

"You're actually driving over there?" Jefferson scoffed.

"Yes! Piper must be mortified. I should have never believed she would cut me out of her life. How could I? I'm not sure what happened Jefferson but promise me you had nothing to do with it."

Jefferson only stared. Keelie's heart sank in disappointment as silence answered her question. Suddenly, the cell phone notification sounded, displaying thirty-three missed calls from Piper. Keelie turned away crossly and exited the room, slamming the door. Jefferson stood motionless, then looked down incredulously at the papers. He knew he had to notify his father.

∞∞∞∞∞∞∞∞∞∞

A sudden and unexpected ringing of the doorbell startled Maya while she prepared lunch for her family.

"Rowe are you expecting someone?"

Rowe didn't answer as she entered the kitchen. She only stopped and stared at the door. Maya felt a sense of unease. She eyed her suspiciously as she wiped her hands on the dish towel and walked across the room to slowly open the door.

She was horrified. It was Keelie.

"Keelie, you're going to get into a world of trouble," Maya warned.

"No, I'm not, Maya. There was a mistake. I'm not sure what happened, but I have Piper's termination papers, and my name is *not* on them. Keelie rushed to her sister and they hugged as their tears flowed. Maya stared at the papers in disbelief. Hearing the commotion, Alfred entered the room. As they looked at the papers together, the chilling realization crept over them. They both knew what had happened. Rowe had changed the story. She was now an adult and officially a Righter.

∞∞∞∞∞∞∞∞∞∞

Jefferson Jenroe sat alone in his vast private quarters at the House of Missions, with his head collapsed in his hands. He was in shock. Somehow, his wife's name had been removed from the termination papers. Completely baffled, he stood and nervously began to pace back and forth as his anger grew. He had to wrap his head around what had happened.

I know I added Keelie's name. I watched Piper sign the papers without ever noticing. How am I going to explain this to my family? They aren't going to be happy about this, especially Father.

"How did this happen?" he roared as he violently struck the lamp off the bedside table, shattering it to pieces.

∞∞∞∞∞∞∞∞∞∞

President Jeremy Jenroe tapped his pen on the expansive

oak desk and stared impatiently at his son.

"I cancelled a meeting this afternoon. What is it that's so urgent?"

"Father, it's the termination papers." Jefferson fidgeted with a loose thread on his sleeve. "I'm absolutely positive that Keelie's name was on these papers. I added it myself. I'm not sure what happened, but I'm convinced there's more to this. Someone had to have changed these papers while Keelie and I were sleeping. *Something* happened."

Jefferson hesitantly placed the papers on the expansive oak desk. Jeremy coolly looked them over.

"Son," he said, "have a seat. There's something I must share with you. Have you ever heard of a Righter?"

"Well, no, Father. I can't say I have."

President Jenroe leaned back and laced his hands behind his head. "Righters are a group of people born with a special gift. They have the ability to rewrite history and even write the future, among other talents."

Jefferson eyed his father in shock, then broke out in a chuckle.

"Father, seriously?"

The president stared, emotionless.

Jefferson's smile faded. "How could this be? If this is even remotely true, then who are these people?"

Jeremey leaned forward. "They can be anyone, son. They are born with a distinctive birthmark that identifies them. My great-grandfather first discovered this when he was in office. However, his tactic was to immediately annihilate them at birth. Clearly, he did not wish to chance one of these individuals changing the success of our leadership. However, as time went on, my grandfather and father took a more humane approach. We now identify them at birth and immediately send them to the orphanages of Exilium. There they never learn to read or write; therefore, they never discover their true talent.

"Are their families aware that their children have these talents?" Jefferson asked.

"Of course not. The only cases we have a hard time explaining are the ones who are rightfully born into the appropriate families. We have those covered by falsified melanin detectors."

Jefferson frowned, taking in his words. "What do you mean by falsified melanin detectors? Does that mean the Medical

Mission is aware of this?"

"Yes, many of them are, but only the ones with top government clearance. They are trained to not utilize the melanin detectors until after the child has been checked for a mark. Of course, there will be some obvious cases that a child is a Sunz, a Metisse, or a Paler. However, when the child's birth traits are not obvious, and if a mark is detected, the Mission doctors have strict orders to utilize the false melanin detector, which will give an immediate reading of Sunz. These children are then sent to the orphanage in Exilium. Unfortunately, there is always the rare chance that a mark is missed or even undetectable the first few weeks of life."

"So, are you saying that there are Righters out there who we may not know about?" Jefferson asked.

"Very well could be." Jeremy eyed his son and lowered his voice. "So, Jefferson, I'm going to ask you, and I'm only going to ask once. I need you to look me in the eye and tell me the absolute truth."

Seconds of silence hovered between them, long enough for Jefferson to notice a subtle hint of anger spark in his father's eyes.

"Go on, Father."

"Could Keelie be a Righter?"

"Absolutely not!" Jefferson raged. "How dare you, Father. If my wife had such a mark anywhere on her body, I would know!" He stood abruptly as his heart pounded. "If you're asking me, I would suspect General Pense!"

"General Pense?" Jeremy frowned.

"Well, yes," Jefferson continued. "He loves that girl and would do anything for her."

President Jenroe leaned back in his chair, pensively gazing out the window. The silence was too much for Jefferson.

"Dad, you have to know it's not Keelie!"

"Hold on, son . . . your thoughts on Alfred Pense . . . you may be onto something. I first suspected something when he became a general. I would have never signed off on that. We figured it was a mix up in the announcements on awards day, but it worked in my favor, so I let it be. He's a well-respected man in Righting."

The president paused again, but when his words came, they were resolute. "Therefore, it's going to be very unfortunate when they lose him. Give the Militia orders to immediately arrest the Penses."

"What about the girl?" Jefferson asked.

"Send her to Exilium!"

A look of horror came over Jefferson. "Please, Father, Keelie will never forgive me."

"Keelie will be fine," President Jenroe coldly replied as he locked eyes with Jefferson. "She will have no choice."

Chapter 10∞
Keelie's Surprise

Feeling quite ill, Keelie returned to the House of Missions that evening. The queasiness had overcome her suddenly at the Penses home that morning. Though she had felt hints of it over the past several days, she attributed it to the emotional roller coaster she had been on. The sudden and violent onset of it today, however, had her picking up her cell and calling her friend and personal physician, Dr. Dara Cleary. Keelie had met Dara in medical school, and the two had remained friends since.

"Hey, Dara, this is Keelie. I haven't been feeling very well lately. Can I get in to see you? It may be the medication you gave me."

Keelie looked around the room to make sure Jefferson was not close by.

"Can you squeeze me in tomorrow morning? Oh no, don't come here, I'll come to you. Okay. See you then. Thanks."

∞∞∞∞∞∞∞∞∞∞

After going through what seemed like a battery of tests, Dr. Dara Cleary re-entered the examination room, admittedly baffled. "Well, Keelie, it looks like you're going to be just fine. I have to inform you that you do not have a stomach bug. You are pregnant."

Keelie felt the color drain from her face. "Did you say pregnant?"

"Yes, Mrs. Jenroe, you are about to make Jefferson a proud papa," said Dara, busily tidying up the room for the next patient while they chatted. "So, you decided against taking the birth control you requested? I have to say, I'm a bit surprised. You were so adamant about not getting pregnant and keeping it a secret from Jefferson and his family. You know, I . . ."

"No," Keelie whispered. "I've been taking it. I've been taking it faithfully. Dara? What happened?"

Dara turned and looked at her nervously.

"May I see your pills?"

Keelie pulled the pill dispenser out of the pouch in her bag and handed it to her. Dara frowned.

"What is it?" Keelie insisted.

"Keelie, they're on to you," Dara whispered. "Someone switched the pills. These are not the pills I gave you. This is a placebo. Someone meant for you to get pregnant.

"I can't . . . I just can't . . ." Keelie sobbed.

"Unfortunately, now, Keelie," Dara said softly, "you have no choice."

∞∞∞∞∞∞∞∞∞∞

Within the walls of the eerily silent House of Missions, Keelie quietly sobbed. After some time, the door of her bedroom edged open. An alarmed Jefferson stood there, shocked to see his wife sobbing with red, swollen eyes.

"Keelie, why are you crying?" He rushed to her side to console her.

"I'm pregnant," she snapped, wiping her red, swollen eyes and composing herself.

"You're what? Oh, Keelie, that's great news! Keelie, I'm going to be a father! We have to tell the family tonight at dinner."

One look at her and it was clear to him that she did not share in his elation.

"Keelie, honey, this is great news. I mean we've been trying, so why are you sad?"

"There's nothing I want more than to have your child, Jefferson, but I can't bear the thought of possibly having to give the child up, no matter what he or she looks like."

Jefferson pulled away. He stood up as his anger mounted.

"You can't say that, Keelie! Especially not here. What's getting into you? You could ruin us with that type of thinking. The law is the law, and we have to follow it. It was the Jenroe family who made this law, and you are now a Jenroe. I expect you to act and think like a Jenroe."

Silence hovered between them, and Keelie refused to flinch at his tone.

"Furthermore, there is no chance that you will give birth to a Sunz," he continued, softening his voice and sitting back down to embrace her. "If by chance we do, then we will happily give it to a loving Sunz family and try again. Do you understand me, Keelie? You have to let this go and know that we are going to have a beautiful little Paler who looks just like you. Just like my beautiful Keelie."

Keelie felt a different nausea churn in her stomach. Stiffly, she returned his embrace as a cloud of worry and questions overcame her.

Had Jefferson switched the pills? She wished she could study his face as he gently rubbed her back. *Was he donning a sinister smirk, or was he sincere?*

She couldn't do it. She felt herself melt at his touch. She couldn't make herself believe for one second that Jefferson would ever betray her so deeply. He loved her. She needed to keep believing it. At that single thought, she pulled him even closer. Someone else had made the switch. Someone in the Jenroe family was on to her. Jefferson was all she had to protect her, and she needed him now more than ever.

Chapter 11∞
Without a Trace

Rowe went out for an early morning jog. She had hoped to clear her head, but unfortunately, it wasn't working. The more she ran, the more her mind raced. Someone had changed those papers. Someone had added Keelie. Adding to her emotions, the fierce anger she had harbored the night before had given way to guilt. She couldn't shake the constant nagging in the back of her mind—those sermons from Maya about doing the right thing. No matter how much she tried to convince herself that changing the termination papers was the right thing to do, she couldn't help but worry that she had put herself and her entire family in danger.

She glanced down at her watch. 7:30 AM. She'd been running over an hour, much longer than planned, and didn't want to miss time with her dad before he left for work. She sprinted the last quarter mile back to the house but stopped short. The front door was wide open. Hesitantly, she stepped in. No smell of breakfast greeted her.

"Hey, I'm back!"

The house was eerily quiet. She stepped through the door. Tousled furniture and broken glass were scattered throughout the living room.

"Mom? Dad?" Her heart pounded.

No one answered her. She raced back to the door and looked to the driveway. Her mom's car was still there. Panicked, she ran to garage entrance. Her dad's black Escalade sat parked in its usual spot. Rowe called for her parents again and again, searching through the entire house. Each room was a disheveled mess, with evidence of a violent scuffle. Her dad's office was destroyed.

As she stood in the hallway in disbelief, she smelled an odor coming from the kitchen. Slowly and cautiously, she returned to find a pot on the stove that had boiled dry. She frantically picked up the phone and called Keelie.

Fourth ring . . .

Oh please, no! Not voicemail . . .

"This is Keelie Jenroe. Leave a message."

Rowe rushed out the door, breaking into a run toward her neighbor's home. She banged furiously on the door. No answer. Out of the corner of her eye, she saw movement. When she looked, she caught sight of her neighbors blatantly closing the blinds.

"Wait, Wait! She begged, rushing to the window. Her heart beat fiercely. "Have you seen my parents?"

She darted from house to house within her block. It became apparent no one was going to speak to her. Reluctantly, she returned home, entering slowly, yet cautiously, careful not to step on the broken glass that covered the floor. She had to calm herself.

Breathe. Relax. Think.

She walked toward her parent's room, navigating more broken glass and overturned furniture on the way. Maybe there would be an intimation as to what had transpired. Her parent's bedroom was no exception to the rest of the house. Drawers were pulled out, and the closet door had been completely pulled off.

"What happened here?" she wondered aloud.

Feeling hopeless, she collapsed on the bedroom floor. As

her eyes surveyed the room, her gaze stopped on the closet. She cocked her head at the odd sight. Cascading out of it, within her reach, was a stack of letters. Someone had purposely gone through each of them.

In a flurry of desperation, she reached for one, hoping it would contain a clue as to what had happened to her parents. It was clearly addressed to Maya Bellows, but the address was not the home in which they currently resided.

Wow, this must be really old. Why would Mom hold on to these old letters?

Rowe's hands shook as she read. This letter didn't have anything in it that would help her find her parents. Curiously, though, based on the handwriting, it was clearly addressed to a very young Maya, from either a family member or a childhood friend, not much older than five. Despite her desperation to find clues, she still had the feeling she was invading her mother's privacy. But she read on. There might be something in one of them that would lead her to her parents.

DEAR MAYA,

I JUST WANT YOU TO KNOW

THAT I MISS YOU SO MUCH. I
CAN'T WAIT TO SEE YOU ON YOUR
NEXT VISIT. THEY HAVE SO
MUCH PLANNED FOR US TO DO.
YESTERDAY, PAMMY HELD A BIBLE
STUDY HERE IN THE HOUSE. IT
WAS NO FUN WITHOUT YOU. I
CAN'T WAIT FOR YOU TO COME
BACK. REMEMBER WHAT PAMMY
ALWAYS SAYS TO US ABOUT
UNITY AND FORGIVENESS
ALWAYS.

I LOVE YOU WITH ALL MY
HEART,

YSTP

Rowe's heart sank. Why hadn't her mom ever discussed her childhood? She felt a pang of guilt. Why hadn't she ever taken the time to ask her about it? This was the first time she had come across any clue that her mother was ever a child. Her hands felt clammy as she held the letter.

Something suddenly dawned on her. Could her mother have come from a Paler family somewhere out there? If she had, she never spoke of it. But maybe that's why she didn't. The only thing she had ever mentioned to Rowe was that her grandparents had passed away before she was born. If Rowe ever asked about them, her mother quickly changed the subject. Once, however, she did share with Rowe that she was an only child. As Rowe continued to rummage through the letters, the messages were all the same—a small child missed her friend.

She carefully put the letters back in the box and gently lifted it back on the shelf.

Who is YSTP? Or what does it mean?

A vase crashed to the floor. The deafening sound jolted Rowe from her thoughts. Her fight or flight response kicked in, and she sprang to her feet, only to realize the vase had just rolled off the dresser.

"What am I doing?" she whispered. "I have to find my parents!"

Carefully, she made her way back to the kitchen. How she wished she would encounter her mother there, in front of the stove, just waiting on her. The only thing that greeted her was the pot that she had neglected to handle, continuing to char on the burner. Instinctively, she grabbed it and tossed it into the kitchen sink, bombarding it with water. The blistering pain from the splattering hot water shot up her arms, but simultaneously, another pain seared through her—a thought that left her falling to her knees and sobbing uncontrollably.

"What have I done?!"

The same thoughts raced through her mind over and over…

The termination papers, I changed them. I caused this! What if I'm the reason my parents are missing? I'll never forgive myself . . .

Even through her raging emotions and panic, she could hear Maya's voice in her head, lecturing her about forgiveness.

I'm sorry, Mom. I'm so sorry. What have I done?

"Piper Sparrow?" She jolted backward against the door of the kitchen cabinet.

Two Paler men dressed in black suits hovered over her. Guardedly and slowly, she stood up.

"Yes, I'm Piper Sparrow," she said as her muscles tensed.

"We are here under the orders of the Jenroe administration," the burlier one emotionlessly announced. "You must come with us."

"Where are my parents?"

"No questions, Miss Sparrow. You are allowed to gather a few personal items, and then you must come with us."

Rowe's heart beat so fast she felt her chest would explode. Her father had warned her against the practice of righting. She had defied him. Did the administration know? Had she put her family in danger just to keep Keelie in her life? She knew she had to remain calm. She had to find a way to escape.

"Give me minute," she softly spoke, as she calmly walked into her bedroom. "I have to put on something warm."

Once in her room, her survival instincts kicked in. Frantically, she paced back and forth. *What am I going to do?*

Then, suddenly, the card on her bedside table caught her eye.

DiCaprio. You will know how to find me when the time is right.

She grabbed a sheet of paper and began writing.

"Hurry, in there!" one of the men bellowed.

She wrote her final words and the portal appeared. Startled by the voice, she stuffed the paper in her jacket and rushed through the portal. Seconds later, the men charged into the empty room. She had outmaneuvered them.

Maya and Alfred Pense, however, had not been so lucky…

∞∞∞∞∞∞∞∞∞

The portal led to a dark, smoky cave. As Rowe entered it, the cold air chilled her to bone. A strong musty smell invaded her nostrils. This didn't look much like the story she had written, but she had written it frantically, without much time.

I have to keep going.

Walking further, she noticed that the walls were lined with religious relics and depictions from the Bible. She caught a glimpse of a sad depiction of Jesus on the cross. Small fires illuminated the cave and warmed groups of people huddled by them. As she walked by, most of them paid her no notice as they struggled to keep warm, while others approached her, begging. A few simply stared. Suddenly, a strange woman with dark hair appeared from nowhere and began walking in front of her.

"Follow me," the woman said as she doubled her speed through the dark cave. "We've been expecting you."

"Hey, slow down!" Rowe said, breaking into a mild sprint to keep up. Something about the mysterious woman seemed just as familiar to Rowe as it did strange. She wasn't exactly sure what, whether it was something about the way the woman moved or whether it was the way she held her head. The swiftness and agility that the woman displayed as she navigated the narrow tunnels of the cave, made it hard for Rowe to keep up. She was unsure of why she was even trusting her, but her instincts urged her on.

"Hey, slow down! Rowe pleaded. "Where are you taking me? And who do you mean by 'we'?"

The woman did not answer. She continued to precipitously maneuver through the tunnels as if their lives depended on it.

"I'm looking for DiCaprio," Rowe continued, breathlessly. "How do I find him?"

The woman only continued to dart expertly through the passages.

"I am looking for DiCaprio!" she angrily repeated, finally catching up. "Can you help me?"

"He is awaiting your arrival," the woman coldly replied. She suddenly stopped and turned toward what seemed like just the wall of the cave. "You'll need to move closer because . . ."

Rowe's attention trailed off as she leaned over, hands on her knees, panting to catch her breath. She frowned.

There it was again. What is it about her? How do I know this woman? . . .

Rowe gasped. *It's her voice. . .*

The woman pressed a button on the wall of the cave. It suddenly opened up into an elevator. The woman grabbed her by the arm and yanked her in as the doors of the elevator abruptly closed. Rowe's stomach took a startling plunge with the sudden jerk of the rapid downward descent.

"Where are we going?" Rowe's voice quavered.

"Just trust me. You will know everything soon enough. My name is Visera, and I am not the enemy!" she snapped. "That title we reserve for the Jenroes. However, we are well aware of your talent. We have known for some time."

Suddenly, the elevator opened up into what appeared to be another world. It was unlike anything Rowe had ever seen, an entire room of futuristic technology that could only be found in the most fantastical science fiction books.

Her degree in technological advancement told her that some of the best scientists and engineers had to have been involved in the creation of a room such as this. But where was she? She glanced around the room. Like the walls in the tunnels, the walls in the room were lined with religious relics and historical depictions of war. She had never known the existence of a site of this caliber anywhere in the United Missions. It was more extravagant than any place she had ever encountered, even in Imperium.

As she roamed the room in awe, Visera continued to speak. Rowe couldn't shake the feeling that she recognized her voice. The more the mysterious woman spoke, the more she was convinced this was not her first encounter with Visera. Everything about her demeanor and her voice seemed familiar, but she knew that she had never laid eyes on the woman standing before her.

"You seem impressed," Visera said with a smirk. "Well,

there is much more where this comes from. Feel free to look around. DiCaprio will be with you in a moment."

Rowe could stand it no longer. "Do I know you?"

Visera paused and turned to look at her. She didn't respond and seemed somewhat amused by Rowe's confusion.

Rowe decided to shrug it off, at least for now. She continued to roam the room, which looked more like a high-tech laboratory. Now that her adrenaline was subsiding, she took more detailed notice of her surroundings. She gasped. Adorning the walls of the building was a symbol virtually identical to her birthmark, plated in gold and platinum.

Wow, what is this place?

Mesmerized, she slowly ran her fingers along the outline of the symbol.

"Hello Rowe," said a voice from behind.

Rowe abruptly turned, facing the stranger that she had encountered so many times without any exchange of words. Now, he was standing before her, calling her name.

"DiCaprio?" Rowe asked with a nod. The man before her looked quite different from the stranger she had encountered in the gym and on the steps of Righting Court. He was clean-shaven and clothed in white linen garments. DiCaprio stood before her with outstretched arms.

"Welcome, Miss Sparrow. Your timing is perfect, and we have much to share with you."

Chapter 12∞
The Promise

Keelie Jenroe took in the cool breeze of the morning as she sat in the rose garden of the House of Missions. She felt more relaxed than she had in days.

How could I have ever doubted Jefferson? Maybe having a child won't be so bad. Life would never be so cruel as to allow me to give birth to a beautiful child, only to have it unjustly taken away. Hasn't losing Piper been traumatic enough?

She knew she didn't have all the answers, but she also knew that she had never witnessed more happiness in the House of Missions since she had married Jefferson. The entire family was now excited about the life that she was carrying inside of her. She, too, was beginning to feel excited. She wanted nothing more than to give Jefferson the child he so longed for, but with every positive thought, the nightmare of the Medical Mission coming in and taking her child away caused her to feel sick.

Flashbacks of the night that Piper was stolen from their lives haunted her more frequently than ever. She wondered if her parents relived that night as often as she did.

"Mrs. Jenroe, you have a visitor," the staffer announced, jarring her from her thoughts.

Keelie turned to see her mother, Jana Sparrow, standing above her on the patio of the rose garden. She donned dark glasses, a scarf that completely covered her hair, and a large winter coat, although it was early spring.

"Mom, I wasn't expecting you," she said nervously, greeting her with a kiss on the cheek. "Is everything okay? Are Dad and Patton okay?"

"They're fine, Keelie. Can't a mother visit her daughter every now and then, even if she lives in the House of Missions?"

"Oh, sure, Mom. I didn't mean anything by it. It's just."

". . . rare that I visit," Jana finished for her. "I know, but I cleared it with Madeline, and I decided to surprise you." She looked Keelie over. "Isn't it a little cool for you to be out here with nothing on your arms? You have two to think about now, young lady."

Keelie looked at her mother and warmly smiled. She was actually happy to have her mother there. She had not shared with her the insecurities and fears that she was having about her pregnancy, but just having her there made her feel safe.

"Well, I am really happy you came by, Mom. And don't worry, the sun will be out soon. It's early spring, anyway." Keelie, patted the seat next to her. "Come and sit with me. The roses smell beautiful this time of year."

Jana Sparrow took a seat beside her daughter and slowly unwrapped herself.

"I guess you're right. I may be the one who is a little overdressed. It's really nice out here."

Warm light beamed down through the bright, blue sky, and Jana drew in a slow, deep breath, taking in the fragrant, cool morning air. "This adds a whole new meaning to taking time to smell the roses," she softly said.

They spent a few moments in comfortable silence, enjoying each other and the surroundings.

"Do you come out here often?" Jana finally asked.

"No . . . not very often. Only when I need to clear my head."

"Well, this must be a great place to clear your head." Jana's tone hinted of sadness. She gazed at the sky above them. "It's absolute serenity. Maybe if I had a rose garden like this, I wouldn't need the wine."

An awkward silence followed.

"Why do you need the wine, Mother?" Keelie softly whispered.

Jana shifted in the lounge chair to look at her daughter. For the first time in years, Keelie caught a glimpse of the mother that she had known as a child. Her eyes were sincere, and she clearly had not been drinking.

"I think about her every day, Keelie." Jana's eyes welled up with tears. "Your father and I both do. At least I have the alcohol. He just does the best he can to get through each day. Did you know that he blames himself for that night?"

"Blames himself?" Keelie blurted. "How could Piper being taken away be his fault?"

"No, obviously it wasn't his fault." Jana shrugged, her cheeks wet with tears. "But I never told him that."

Keelie, took a deep breath and listened with attentiveness. Her mother sat before her, crying, and for the first time in years, she was doing so without the comfort of alcohol.

"I was so consumed with my own pain that I allowed your dad to hurt. I allowed him to believe that there was something he could have done to keep Piper in our home. I was selfish, and I what was cruel. I knew it was the law, but I expected your father to spend his life trying to right a wrong that wasn't his fault. Keelie, I was raised by a wonderful mother who taught me forgiveness, but I am a drunk because it eases the pain of not being able to forgive myself."

Keelie leaned over and embraced her Mom as they both silently sobbed.

"It's okay, Mom. Dad loves you," Keelie whispered. "It doesn't matter the law was then or is now, Dad would have blamed himself anyway. That is who he is. He has always wanted to give you the world—me, you, Patton, and even Piper."

Jana's eyes searched Keelie's. "You do know we love Piper, right?"

"Of course, Mom, but it's not me who needs to know . . . Piper needs to know."

"I thought if we accept that this is just the way things are, Keelie, it would make it easier for her. I never meant to make her feel as if we didn't care. That was never my intention. I know my drinking didn't help, but it was the only way I could numb my pain. It was the only way to see her every month and be able to let go again . . . and again, and again."

Keelie looked at her pleadingly. "Did you ever consider telling her the truth, Mom? The whole truth?"

Jana was silent for a few seconds and then met her gaze. "It isn't just my decision, Keelie. There are others with a say-so in how much she learns. Don't you think I wanted to tell her? So many times, when Maya brought her to visit, I wanted to let it all out, but I couldn't. I'd promised. That is the one thing that I have done right in my life. I have kept that promise for many years. It's a promise I made before any of you were born. I will never break it."

Keelie knew the promise her mother spoke of. She pulled her close in a hug and felt her shudder. She squeezed her eyes shut. *Dear God, when my baby arrives, please don't let me experience this same turmoil . . .*

She thought of the promise, the secret that had been kept

from Piper all of her life. She knew that if that secret ever came out, it would destroy what Alfred and Maya had built with Piper.

Most of all, she knew that very secret could destroy them all.

Chapter 13∞
Underground

Rowe was led into a room filled with floating digital monitors that scanned the activities of various areas throughout the territories. "Before we begin, Miss Sparrow, allow me to show you this," DiCaprio said.

Young, yet significantly older than Rowe, DiCaprio's dark eyes sparkled in the light of the room. He was the epitome of the cliché tall, dark, and handsome with chiseled features and a thin, straight nose. Despite his attractive features, he donned an imposing presence and intimidating aura. His olive-colored skin made it difficult for Rowe to decipher if he was a Paler or a Metisse, but one thing was for sure, she couldn't deny that he cleaned up rather well. No longer did he don a scraggly beard but standing before her was a man of debonair character with an immaculately shaved five-day shadow. Admittedly, she no longer found him strange or eerie.

He motioned her towards the various digital screens. Rowe could see all territories, including Imperium. She came to a sudden halt in front of the monitor showing the inside of the House of Missions. She immediately recognized Keelie, alone her room, crying.

"Keelie! That's my sister," Rowe gasped. "Why is she crying?"

DiCaprio didn't answer. He nodded for Rowe to continue moving forward.

"As you should have figured out by now, you and I share a very special gift, Miss Sparrow. I, too, am a Righter."

Rowe only starred at DiCaprio, in awe of all she was taking in. He was correct. She had figured it out. She remembered that day when her curiosity and defiance had forced her to confront her parents about the connection between herself and this strange man with the same mark. The information that Alfred and Maya had given her only confirmed her suspicions. But she still had questions.

"Why am I here?" Rowe anxiously asked. "This place was not in my story. This not what I wrote."

"Piper Sparrow," DiCaprio suddenly spouted, "also known by the nickname, Rowe. You were born March 24, 3016, to Doctors Philmore and Jana Sparrow. Unfortunately, the melanin detector identified you as a Sunz, and you were immediately taken from your family. You were relocated to the home of Alfred and Maya Pense in the Righting territory. There, they discovered a mark on your inner thigh, but at the time there was no knowledge of its significance. Although your father later learned of its significance, he quickly gauged it had been missed by the officials of the Medical Mission when you were born, thereby preventing you from becoming a resident of the orphanages of Exilium. It wasn't until you were 4 years old that you became aware of your own gift, and even then, you did not fully understand it."

"Visera is the head of the psychic mission." DiCaprio gestured towards the mysterious woman who had led the way through the tunnels. "She's a psychic and a shape shifter by gift, but she is not a Righter. She encountered you in the park under the supervision of Maya Pense when you were only an infant. However, upon immediate contact with you, she knew you were a Righter."

Rowe's gaze switched from DiCaprio to Visera. She wasn't sure if she could trust either of them. She was still curious how DiCaprio knew so much about her.

"How do you know all of this? And where are my parents?"

DiCaprio and Visera traded glances as a few seconds of silence passed, then moved on without answering.

"Fortunately, Miss Sparrow," DiCaprio finally spoke, "you are not alone. There are others like you and me. It was Visera who discovered my abilities when I was only a child and ultimately trained me to utilize them.

"Visera trained *you*?" Rowe asked, suddenly turning to face Visera.

Abruptly, Visera walked away. Rowe frowned. There was still something about the familiarity of her. She dismissed it and continued to gaze around the room. Suddenly, the floating digital screens surrounded her. The first screen displayed clear memories of a 5-year-old DiCaprio being trained rigorously by Visera. On the second screen, he was a little older, and by the third screen, he was clearly a teen, and so on. Rowe slowly turned in amazement so as to get a clear view of each screen as they surrounded her. She continued to turn in a dizzying spin as each screen quickly changed from scene to varying scene of DiCaprio's life. However, she was more distracted with Visera on the screens, who appeared much older than her swiftness and agility revealed. Suddenly, the screens disappeared, and Rowe found herself questioning again why she was even there.

"So, if you have known about me since I was a child, why now?"

"Why not now?" DiCaprio said. "To be honest, we have been around since you were a child, preparing you for this day."

"Preparing me?" Rowe snapped. "What do you mean preparing me?"

"Visera, would you please do us the honor?" DiCaprio stepped back and gave Visera a nod.

Slowly, she raised her head and made unnerving eye contact with Rowe. Feeling a sudden sense of unease, along with the perplexing air of familiarity, Rowe shifted her stance and cautiously backed away from her. Then she felt her hair begin to lift on the back of her neck and a chill take over her body as the strange woman she had only just met began to transform before her. With her eyes locked on Visera, Rowe maintained her distance and kept DiCaprio in her periphery, suddenly questioning if she should trust either of them.

"What in the world is going on here?" Rowe demanded in a throaty whisper. She was in complete disbelief. She had never witnessed anything like this in her life. Right before her eyes, Visera was becoming more and more familiar, and within moments, no longer was the mysterious woman standing before her, but the woman who had trained her since she was a child . . .

"*Winnie?*" she questioned, wide-eyed.

"Yes, Miss Sparrow," DiCaprio answered. "This is Winnie. However, Visera is her actual name. Do not be afraid. Visera is a shapeshifter, and she has been a part of your life for a long time.

Rowe remained motionless, in shock. The woman standing before her clearly appeared to be her trainer, Winnie, whom she had known and trusted for years.

"How can I be sure that's Winnie? This woman just changed her entire appearance in front of me."

"Let me handle this, DiCaprio," Winnie said, stepping forward. "Rowe, remember I told you to go after DiCaprio the first time you encountered him?"

Rowe didn't answer immediately. Her mind went back to that day in the gym when Winnie urged her to follow DiCaprio, an unnamed stranger.

"Yes . . . I . . . mean, I remember," Rowe stammered, "but that still does not prove that you are who you say you are. Tell me something else that only you and I would know."

Winnie paused . . . "Your father and I began training you the moment you began walking."

"That doesn't prove anything!" Rowe interrupted.

"Allow me to finish!" Winnie demanded, raising her voice.

A tense silence stood between them. "Go on," Rowe softly challenged. "Prove that you—Visera and Winnie—are one and the same."

"By the time you were 10 years old, you were better than me in your self-defense training," Visera revealed slowly. "However, you never told your father because we had formed a bond, and you didn't want to lose me as a trainer. You made me promise not to tell your father that your skills were well beyond what I could teach you. I honored your request. It has been a secret that we've kept these many years, and for that, I am very grateful."

Rowe found herself at a loss of words. Her shoulders slumped, and her tensed muscles suddenly began to relax.

"Why didn't you tell me?" she asked with sigh.

"It wasn't time," Winnie replied, looking at her earnestly. "However, allow me to introduce myself again.

"Hello, Piper Sparrow, my name is Visera." She suddenly transformed back into the image of the mysterious woman that Rowe had only just met. She extended her hand to Rowe as if meeting her for the first time.

"Hello, Visera," Rowe slowly spoke, grasping the woman's hand while struggling to wrap her head around what had transpired.

She suddenly turned to DiCaprio. "Why now?"

"You have just celebrated your 18th birthday. Unfortunately, it is around the age of 18 that most undetected Righters either do something to get discovered or go completely rogue due to coming-of-age or their parents losing complete control. We have kept an eye on you, as well as several others, over the years. It's very clear that the Penses have raised you well. The recent circumstances of your life, for the most part, have been coincidental. However, we had always planned that you and I would make full contact around your 18th birthday, regardless."

"So, there are others?" Rowe asked.

"Yes," DiCaprio replied. "There are seven of us including both you and I, who we are aware of. However, there may be many others who have no idea. Before we get into that, I must explain. It's imperative that you are fully informed. It will be your choice if you wish to join our mission."

"Fully informed of what?" Rowe interjected.

DiCaprio paused as the room filled with silence. He slowly walked toward Rowe until she could feel his warm breath on her face, but she stood her ground. He looked her in the eyes.

". . .what we are capable of . . . together," DiCaprio continued. "You, I, and the others have the power to initiate the beginning and write the end of the final war to overthrow and decimate Jenroe rule.

The room was silent but for the soft sound of Visera's breathing in the background.

"Would you like for me to continue?" DiCaprio asked.

"Yes," Rowe softly responded. She couldn't think of anything she wanted more than to destroy the Jenroes. "Continue," she said, giving DiCaprio a nod.

"Follow me." He pressed a button on the wall.

Immediately, a wall to the right of the room ascended, opening into a long corridor. The walls of the corridor were a pristine white and lined with panels. As DiCaprio entered the corridor, Rowe and Visera swiftly followed. With a wave of his hand, each panel revealed a floating digital screen that suddenly appeared before them. Rowe caught her breath, in awe as he pointed to the first one.

"This, Miss Sparrow, was our land in the 21st century. In those days, our ancestors lived in what was known as the United States of America."

Beautiful images of the old country Rowe had learned about gleamed right before her on a floating screen. As they continued through the corridor, each floating screen revealed more moving images than Rowe could take in.

"There were fifty individual territories that had existed for well over 200 years," DiCaprio explained as he moved to the next panel which revealed a new screen depicting a map of the entire country.

"This vast country went through its ups and downs, but eventually it became the ultimate symbol for a true democracy throughout the world."

"Yea, that's what Dad tells me." Rowe rolled her eyes. "Apparently the good old United States had global influence."

"Our Country, Miss Sparrow, was not only the most influential, but the strongest country in the world, and the rest of the world looked to us for both leadership and guidance. The majority of our nation practiced Christianity, but for many years we welcomed all from different faiths and backgrounds. We even took in the poor and persecuted. Here is a symbol of that." DiCaprio strolled further down the corridor, revealing yet another floating screen.

"That's an image of Lady Liberty," Rowe softly said.

"Yes," said DiCaprio, quickly moving on toward another panel on the opposite side of the corridor. "However, the inscription has been changed from what it said all those years ago. Read this."

Rowe followed quickly behind DiCaprio and began to read the inscription aloud.

"Give me your tired, your poor, your huddled masses yearning to breathe free, the wretched refuse of your teeming shore. Send these, the homeless, tempest-tossed to me, I lift my

lamp beside the golden door!"

"Unfortunately, it doesn't say that anymore," Rowe replied. "I am assuming that changed with the beginning of the Jenroe rule."

"Unfortunately, you are correct," DiCaprio continued, pointing to an image on yet another floating digital screen. "During the presidential election of 2016, this man came along."

"Murt," Rowe whispered.

"Yes," DiCaprio replied with a raised brow. "So, you know a little history?"

"I guess you could say I'm well-read."

"Do you know the true story then?"

"I learned from my father that Murt betrayed his country. That's all I need to know."

"You are partially correct. However, it's possible that Murt's intention was never to betray the American people. Yes, he made a deal with the enemy, and in those days, depending on which side of the political spectrum you were on, he was either a complete narcissist or a hero. However, what we have learned is that Murt's plans were to double-cross those he appeared to be colluding with, punishing them for the treachery they had planned for his people."

"How do you know all of this?" asked Rowe.

"Follow me." DiCaprio swiftly walked toward the end of the corridor. As he walked, each floating screen disappeared. At the end of the corridor, a steel vaulted door opened, leading the way into yet another room. In wonderment, Rowe took a circumferential gaze of the room. It was filled with a level of technology beyond what she had ever encountered. However, this room only contained one large screen.

"Feast your eyes, Piper Sparrow, as I explain. The beautiful place you see on this screen was the Presidential Resort of Nadold P. Murt. This is where Murt's plan to change everything was concealed the night the United States of America was annihilated."

"What happened?" Rowe asked.

"Murt was like us," DiCaprio said, slowly turning to her. "He was a Righter. He even wrote his win of the election of 2016. Clemens actually won."

Rowe remained silent, displaying a look of disbelief. She nodded, gesturing for DiCaprio to continue.

"His story was in a vault at this place on the screen and so was the portal," DiCaprio continued. "He suspected Petrov and the others would betray him, and he was prepared. All of their secret meetings were held at Par La Mer, so Murt strongly believed that if betrayal were to take place, it would be at Par La Mer. It appears that Murt wrote a story and created a portal that would save the American people. He had fulfilled his promise. The Wall was built. The only thing left to do was to make America superb again . . . just as he had promised. We strongly believe that Murt's deep desire to be a hero for the American people was what actually hurt him in the end. Fate had a different set of plans."

"But what about history?" asked Rowe. "We can't just ignore history. None of this is mentioned. And what do you mean by, 'We believe?' Don't you have any proof?"

"Sort of," said DiCaprio. "The story we have was not complete, so we are not sure what Murt's plans were, or if he was planning to control the ending himself once he entered the portal. Based on the rest of the story, we can only guess."

"What do you mean, 'guess?'"

"Well, it appears that history may have taught us wrong, Rowe," said DiCaprio. "Although we don't have a complete story, based on what we do have, it seems Murt miscalculated when the betrayal would take place. He and his family were not at Par La Mer, as he suspected they would be. They were at the White House when the phone call came in at three in the morning. Par La Mer, unfortunately, was almost a thousand miles from the White House. Murt was trapped. He didn't have time to save his country."

"I can't believe this!" exclaimed Rowe. "He could have just written the outcome. Why wouldn't he do that?"

"I'm not sure," DiCaprio replied. "I have several theories based on the research our team has done. However, any of them could be true. The most plausible ideas are either he didn't have complete control of his Righting abilities, or he thought that he could control the ending without writing it. The latter is more likely, but if so, it seems he was greatly disappointed in the end."

"Hold on DiCaprio!" Rowe interjected. "This is a lot to take in. I'm confused. I was told by my father that my Righting abilities were due to the nuclear emission in the environment after the annihilation. So how was Murt a Righter?"

"That is another falsehood that history tells us. The Jenroe administration would like for us to believe that we exist due to the nuclear emissions left after the annihilation. However, our research shows that Righters have always existed. When the United States of America was a world power, the Righters were a top-secret government program. They were studied and often used as part of national security. There were not many of us. However, it is believed that if any human could withstand a nuclear holocaust . . ."

". . . it would be Righter," Rowe slowly finished for him.

"Yes," replied DiCaprio, "and it is believed that of the few that existed, most, if not all of them, survived. They integrated into the new world and passed their abilities down genetically, creating more people like us, and now after hundreds of years, here we are."

"So, did Murt survive?" Rowe asked.

"No," replied DiCaprio, "but it is my belief that he did not want to because he could not face the American people, or it could simply be that he did not wish to live without his family."

"How do you know so much?" asked Rowe.

DiCaprio motioned above Visera. He reached up and pulled a lever just above his head. A clear tubular apparatus descended. He reached in and pulled out several documents bound into one.

"All of your answers are here," he said, handing the documents to Rowe. "These are Murt's writings."

Rowe eyed the bound documents in disbelief. She looked up at DiCaprio. "*How*... where did you get these?"

"The vault at Par La Mer," said DiCaprio. "As I told you, we have been working for years in search of the truth, and we now have many of the answers. Unfortunately, during early Jenroe rule, they uncovered classified information detailing the top-secret Righter's program. A horrible atrocity took place soon after. All Righters were supposedly identified by these classified documents. There was a government order put out to gather all the Righters. Over 6 million innocent men, women and children were gathered and slaughtered. This event in history is missing from our history books, Rowe. It is called the Great Gathering."

"How do we not know about this?" Rowe asked, as her heart pounded.

"They do not wish for us to know, but we have footage. I just don't think you're ready for it yet. However, once they realized that the annihilation did not kill us all, and that the gathering did not identify us all, they erased it from the history books. And there was a good reason for this. Should they elect to carry out another gathering, we would never see it coming."

DiCaprio pressed another button. The wall ascended, opening to the original room in which Rowe had entered. Once again, she found herself standing in front of a floating digital screen that was displaying continuous scenes of the old America— the United States of America. She stood in veneration. She had never experienced anything as beautiful in the United Missions as what she was seeing on that screen.

"Rowe, we have the power to change all of this," DiCaprio whispered. "We have the power to finish what Murt started."

"But . . ." Rowe interrupted, feeling overwhelmed.

"But what?" DiCaprio anxiously probed.

Rowe paused as she turned to face him.

"I never knew it was so beautiful. I mean, not just aesthetically, but the concept. I never knew so many different people lived in harmony. How could one person destroy all of that?"

"Well, it wasn't perfect," DiCaprio replied. "Just as in any civilization, there were the 'haves' and 'have-nots,' but the opportunities were there. The level of oppression and injustice was nowhere near what we are experiencing with the Jenroe administration. And this is only the beginning. They have plans for us, Rowe."

Visera walked over and joined DiCaprio. "But, not only have we been doing our homework," she added. "We have been spying on the Jenroes for quite some time."

DiCaprio moved to another floating digital screen.

"She's right," he said. "This is what we've learned. Over the next five years, the administration plans to build a wall around Imperium. This alleged wall will lock out all the other territories."

"Well, that's a good thing, isn't it?" Rowe asked. "Then the remaining territories can unite, and we can govern ourselves."

Visera shook her head. "Although it sounds good, their plan is to destroy us," she said. "We do not know how, but Jenroe knows that the only people who can change this are the Righters."

"And," DiCaprio added, "He's not afraid, because all the known Righters, withstanding both you and me, were exiled to Exilium. There they are not allowed to learn to read and write. Remember, many of them have no idea they have this gift. However, Visera predicted that there were four others who were fully literate with exceptional aptitude and abilities. She was right. We found them, Rowe, and we convinced them to join our cause.

We had to locate them before the Jenroe administration realized they existed. Alfred Pense has protected you well. Unfortunately, it is to his own detriment that he has protected you."

In the flurry of events, Rowe had nearly forgotten about her parents. The weight of their disappearance came crashing back down on her.

"What do you mean?" asked Rowe.

"You changed your story," DiCaprio said. She noticed the edge of frustration in his voice. "You removed your sister's name from the termination papers. Jefferson Jenroe added your sister's himself. They knew the only way that list could have been changed was by a Righter. They suspect Alfred Pense. They've suspected him ever since he became a brigadier general. However, they purposely did nothing about it as they realized it worked in their favor. If a Sunz was a leader, it would help to keep order in Righting."

"They suspect *Dad?*" Rowe cried out.

"Yes," replied DiCaprio, "and it needs to stay that way for now."

"What do you mean? Where is he? Where are my parents?"

DiCaprio nodded gesturing Rowe to swipe through another floating screen that suddenly appeared. As Rowe swiped through the territories, he explained to her that she could scroll back through in time to earlier in the morning and choose an exact address to view. Rowe had to know what happened to her parents.

As she studied the floating screen, Rowe carefully chose 6:00 a.m. She could see herself leaving her home in Righting and jogging away, oblivious to the militia vehicle pulling into the drive as she jogged further and further away.

Three men forcefully entered their home. Maya and Alfred Pense did not resist. They were immediately restrained while the men tore through the Pense home, destroying Alfred's office and all the other rooms just as she had found things when she returned from her jog later that morning. Rowe sat there watching the men take her parents away.

"Where did they take them?" she demanded.

DiCaprio initiated another floating screen depicting the United Missions primary military base in Righting. As the screen zoomed into a basement room, Rowe slowly sank down against the wall. A cry escaped her lips. Alfred Pense lay on the floor, unconscious and severely beaten.

Chapter 14∞
The Wronged and the Righters

As the militia men descended the cold stone stairs into the dark depths of the underground prison cell in Righting Court, an ominous echo rang out, chilling a barely conscious Alfred Pense to the bone. With each foreboding step in his direction, the impact of the guards' clunky boots yielded an unspoken warning that he was surely about to meet his fate. *Clunk, clunk, clunk,* the boots sounded, as if taking deliberate steps to announce his doom. He couldn't see a thing. Not a hint of light seared through the dark abyss in which he had been thrown. However, he could clearly gauge that the guards were returning to his cell as the clunking against the stone stairs grew with increasing intensity. Alfred was not sure how far away the militia men were, but he readied himself for the fight of his life.

He had to save his family, even if it meant losing his own life in doing so.

It was not long before the blinding glow of the guard's flashlight beamed excessively above him. He could hear the murmurs of the guards discussing his demise but couldn't see their faces. As brigadier general over many men, it was impossible to be familiar with the voices of all his subordinates, yet he thought there should be at least a tinge of familiarity in the voices of the two men sent to escort him to his doom.

"General Pense," the first guard called out.

Alfred didn't move. He wasn't incapacitated, despite having been beaten badly, but he wasn't about to let on that he still had a fighting chance. As he remained motionless, straining to identify their voices, a soft moan escaped him.

"General Pense," the young man called out again. "I have been sent to move you."

"We're going to have to help him," said the other guard with urgency. "He's taken a severe beating. If we're going to do this, we must do it quickly before they get back, or they'll surely kill him."

Alfred felt a ray of hope, but kept up his defenses.

"Who are you?" he demanded, guarding his eyes against the insult of the blinding flashlight.

"First Sergeant Packard, at your service," the young man replied with a salute.

"At ease, Sergeant," Alfred replied. He moaned again.

"Sir, are you okay?"

"It depends on whose asking?" Alfred growled as he pushed himself upright on the stone floor of the prison cell.

"We're here to help sir. But we must get you out of here quickly. Are you able to walk?"

"Yes, I am able to walk!" Alfred snapped, "but I'm not going anywhere until I know that my wife and my daughter are safe. Do you know where they are?"

"Yes sir, they are safe," Packard assured. "We have already moved the other prisoners, sir, and now we have to get you out."

"How can I be sure that I can trust you?"

"Sir, you have no choice. Now we must get you out of here now, or we'll all be prisoners."

"I demand to know who sent you!" Alfred barked.

"Sir, please!" Packard pleaded, lowering his voice. "Someone may hear you. We must make it appear that you escaped. Trust us, please. There's been a safe exit prepared for you. Everything will be explained once you reach your destination safely."

"How will I know when and if I am safe?"

"Visera sent us!" the man replied.

General Pense did a double take. He had not heard the name Visera for quite some time. He only knew her now as Winnie. Slowly, with much effort, he raised himself the rest of the way. He knew he could trust the men, and he knew if Visera had sent a team for him, he would be okay. The men grabbed him on either side under his arms and practically carried him as they swiftly led him to freedom. He couldn't believe his luck . . . or, as his wife would say, his blessings.

Carefully, they scaled the dark stairwell that had led to the depths of the prison cells in Righting Court. Packard led the way with the dull beam of a lone flashlight in his possession. Alfred was very familiar with the guard assignment of Righting Court.

"Where are the other guards?" Alfred demanded.

"There was a change of shift sir."

"Well, then, we must hurry," said Alfred. "There will be a general coming any second to check whether the perimeter guard is secured."

"Yes sir," Packard replied as he continued to lead the way.

As they approached the top of the stairwell, the bright light of the sun pierced Alfred's eyes.

"We must be careful," Alfred warned. "We've reached the open court. Is the perimeter not heavily guarded?"

"No sir," Packard replied. "We were the ones assigned to the perimeter at the change of the shift. There is only one other guard, and we told him that we were given orders to relocate a prisoner. He won't be suspicious. The portal is located just outside the gate. If we can reach the portal without being discovered, you will be safe and with the others immediately."

A sudden whirl wind blew an enormous gust of dust and wind as they struggled to make their way across Righting Court. Sweat dripped down Alfred's face as he eyeballed Packard grasping the butt of his weapon, secured at his waist. Led by the young militia man, Alfred cautiously crossed the dusty open court. He was in pain but walked as swiftly as he could. Everything in him screamed, "*Run, run toward the portal.*", but he dismissed the thought. As a brigadier general, he was sure he could normally overpower any of the others who attempted to thwart his escape, but not in his current condition.

"Packard!" a gruff, familiar voice called out from across the court yard. Packard glanced back. Alfred didn't turn. The man stepped past the archway and entered into the court.

"Where are you taking this prisoner?" The man demanded.

Packard stood, frozen, unsure how to respond.

"Answer me!"

Alfred recognized the voice of General Scarfold. He quickly whispered, "Tell him General Tillman ordered you to move me!"

"Sir, I am moving this prisoner on the orders of General Tillman," Packard announced.

His voice was shaky, and Alfred was sure they would be discovered. Scarfold had been quite a nemesis throughout Alfred's military career.

"Tillman, you say?" Scarfold suspiciously questioned.

"Yes, sir!" Packard answered, now more self-assured.

"Why are there only two of you?" the general demanded. "Do you realize that this man is a brigadier general? He could easily overpower both of your numbskulls and confiscate your weapons."

Alfred held his stance. Scarfold knew exactly who he was. As Alfred suspected, Scarfold was deeply involved in the arrest of his family.

"Yes sir!" replied Packard. "The prisoner is highly incapacitated. We assessed the risk thoroughly before moving him."

"Okay, soldier, if you're confident you can handle this," Scarfold replied with a cold stare. "I will hold you to it. I am assuming that you are moving him to the east side of Righting Court. However, if anything goes wrong, you will be held accountable, and there will be severe consequences."

"Yes sir!" Packard replied with a salute.

Scarfold returned the salute. "Carry on."

Alfred breathed a deep sigh of relief and felt weak as Scarfold turned to go in the opposite direction.

"The portal is just outside of the gate," Packard frantically whispered.

Alfred mustered his strength. "I am assuming you will be joining us, too?" he asked.

"Scarfold has spotted us moving you, so now we have no

choice," said Packard.

As they reached the gate, Alfred clearly saw the portal in the distance, a blurred doorway that suddenly appeared, beckoning their entry.

"Hold it there, soldier!" a voice bellowed.

Alfred pivoted toward the voice. "It's Tillman!" he yelled. "Through the portal, now!"

∞∞∞∞∞∞∞∞∞∞

Rowe was terrified. The screen with the images of her dad went black. "We have to go get him!" she gasped. "We have to go get him now."

"I have men working on that," DiCaprio reassured, calmly. "We have insiders. It is too dangerous for you. They are looking for you, Rowe, and they may now suspect you are the Righter. And by the way, Miss Sparrow, you did not write your escape today."

Rowe was wide-eyed. "What?"

DiCaprio smiled. "I did. I wrote your escape this morning. Getting you to write was just an added touch. I left the window open in my story, so they believe you escaped through the window. They have blocked off all routes out of Righting."

Rowe felt a tinge of violation in DiCaprio's control over her. "Where is my mother?" she snapped.

"Your mother is safe. She's in Exilium," DiCaprio continued as he initiated more screens that displayed the events of the morning. "Others have been exiled."

Rowe drew a sharp breath. "Harper!" The screen depicted his capture that morning. "Why would they exile Harper?"

"The Jenroes found documents in your dad's office this morning implicating Harper," replied DiCaprio. "It seems the documents date back over 10 years. They show Harper attempting to convince your father to join a cause against the administration. Alfred clearly turned him down. That is the only thing that saved him from first-degree sedition. Harper was immediately arrested and exiled this morning, and, thankfully, the Jenroe's are doing our work for us."

"What do you mean doing *your* work?" asked Rowe. "Why would you want Harper arrested?"

"The cause that Harper was speaking of is our cause," DiCaprio explained. "However, he was careful not to reveal it in the communication. Harper hired you because he was fully aware of what you were capable of. He even asked you to write, didn't he?"

Rowe paused, thinking back on the excessive number of times Harper approached her about writing.

DiCaprio placed his hand on Rowe's shoulder. "Harper is here with us. We are located in a secret underground headquarters built for our cause, directly below Exilium. Thankfully, the Jenroe administration would never expect anyone in Exilium to be able to pull off such an elaborate plan. They have no idea we exist."

"How could the Jenroes not know that such an intricate plan was underway, right under their noses? How can you be sure the Jenroes have no idea?"

"As I said," DiCaprio reiterated, "we have insiders. They are loyal. That is how we have access to many areas in various territories. We were considering Keelie, but the Jenroes have placed a road block in those plans."

"How so?" asked Rowe.

"See for yourself," said DiCaprio as he showed Rowe footage of Keelie's morning.

"She's pregnant?" Rowe disappointingly whispered.

"Yes," replied DiCaprio, "but through no choice of her

own. She was secretly taking birth control. The Jenroe's discovered her deceit and switched her pills with a placebo. Keelie is very brave. However, bringing her on board would be too dangerous. We refuse to put any child in danger. So, we'll have to find another way. It was one of our inside operatives that assisted Keelie. Thankfully, she escaped this morning. She's here with us now. As soon as we realized the Jenroe's had switched Keelie's pills, we wrote Dara out of Imperium and brought her here with us. Dara was born in the Metisse territory, she is of Hispanic descent, but she was removed from her home when she was born because she appeared to be a Paler. She and your sister met in medical school and became best friends."

"Yes," said Rowe, "I've heard Keelie talk about her."

"Well, she shared her story with Keelie, and that is why they became so close. Keelie in turn, shared her story about losing you. That's why Keelie felt she could trust Dara to help her."

Suddenly, Dr. Dara Cleary stepped into the room.

"Hello, Rowe," she said.

"Hi," Rowe responded. Her head was spinning. She abruptly turned to DiCaprio. "Well, where do we go from here? What do we do?"

"We have a group out now to retrieve your father," DiCaprio replied. "As for your mother, she's safe where she is. She's with a family that is a part of a covert sub operative we call the underground passage. This provides food, clothing, and secretive literacy to the people of Exilium. The administration has no idea we have books there. The classes are held in a new area that is top secret. This, too, is underground. We have managed to increase literacy in Exilium residents by 80 percent. Our goal is to identify if there is even a small chance that any other Righters exist. That includes the ones who were never taught to read and write. If there are more, we need to get them trained extensively. If we can manage this, then we will have an army that the Jenroes will never be able to defeat."

"What about the unidentified Righters with the marks like us?" Rowe asked. "How do we find them?"

"Hold on, young lady. Before I go any further, I must inform you that as a Righter, you have more gifts than you have discovered," said DiCaprio. "Rowe, you have fortunately mastered the gift of writing the story, but Righters are capable of far more."

"What other gifts are you talking about?" Rowe asked.

DiCaprio grinned. "Many additional gifts, my dear. You, Miss Sparrow, along with the rest of us, have the gift of morphing, mind reading and control, fire initiation and control, levitation, flight, and the ability to control and communicate with nature, among other gift that we may have yet to discover."

Rowe stared, slack jawed. "You have got to be kidding me!"

"No, I'm actually being quite honest. Have you not noticed how easily you perform certain defense moves? Do you notice how you seem . . . how should I say . . . light on your feet?"

Rowe thought for a moment. "Well, yes, but . . ."

"But, those gifts are not your mastered skill," DiCaprio interrupted. "Trust me, we will work on them. Each of the Righters that we have discovered thus far has a different skill which he or she has mastered. You, my dear, as I've said before, are my master story writer with the highest level of militia skills."

DiCaprio suddenly moved to another floating screen. On it, four faces appeared.

"Here we have Connor Spaulding, Jenna Davis, Xander Romanov, and Princley Kerr. All four of these individuals are literate Righters. Like you, they all went undiscovered by the medical mission at their birth. Connor is a third-degree black belt. Although he's fairly proficient in the art of story writing, his mastered skill is mind reading and control."

Rowe glared at the screen. "He's a Paler."

"Yes, but an orphan. He was born with the mark, and although his past is sketchy, he is loyal. Connor showed up on the Exilium landscape in the last decade when he was just a teenager. He was a crash survivor with complete memory loss. Visera was brought in to identify him, and she confirmed that he was an orphan. She sensed that he was a Righter who at some point had known his abilities, so she helped him to rediscover and develop his talent.

Thankfully, Connor could read and write. Being that he is a Paler, it our strong belief that his Paler family was hiding his mark from the Jenroe administration. We also believe that he may have been sent to Exilium as an orphan as he was not a documented Righter.

As I told you before, there may be other Righters with the mark in Exilium, but none of them are literate, and unfortunately, their talents were not developed. We are learning that if some part of gift has not been discovered while the Righter is a child, it may never develop. So far, we have discovered hundreds with the mark, but no sign of Righter talents."

"Where is Connor now?" Rowe asked.

"He is here with us. Thankfully, he is a technological genius and has made much of this possible."

"Jenna Davis looks familiar," Rowe whispered as she turned her attention to another face on the screen.

DiCaprio smiled. "She should. She lives in Righting. Jenna is a fifth-degree black belt with amazing archery skills. She can flawlessly control the actions and thoughts of animals and nature itself. She's a little older than you and attended public school, so no doubt you've seen her in passing numerous times."

"What about the other two?" asked Rowe.

"They are in Metisse. They should arrive in the morning. Their marks are in discrete places, and it is only pure luck that they escaped detection. There was no way for these families to know that these discrete birthmarks had some larger meaning that would make their children a walking target for the Jenroe administration. However, like you, they, too, discovered their gifts at a young age."

"So, how *did* you find them?" asked Rowe.

"Visera, of course," DiCaprio replied. "Thanks to her psychic abilities. Once the children discover their own abilities, then Visera can discover them. Finding you as an infant was just sheer luck. However, along with the sub operatives in Metisse, she then informs the families what their children's marks mean, and precautions are immediately taken to keep the children safe and hidden from the Jenroe Administration. Fortunately, just like she trained you, she immediately began training the others as well, once their talent had surfaced. You have all remained undiscovered.

The Righters in Metisse know each other and have made contact. Fortunately, they are fully on board with our plan. Xander Romanov is a priceless addition to this group. He is a fourth-degree black belt and can create explosive fires with the slightest thought."

"What about the girl? Rowe queried. "She looks more like a beauty pageant contestant than a Righter."

"Oh, my dear, do not judge a book by its cover." DiCaprio's eyes flashed with pride. "This is Miss Princley Kerr, and she has flight and levitation down to a science. Unfortunately, she is only a first-degree black belt, but we have someone to help us with that, and he should be arriving any minute."

There was silence for a moment as Rowe took in all the information DiCaprio shared.

"Who's supposed to be there?" Rowe asked, suddenly noticing the blank spot. "You said there were seven of us all together. I take it you haven't been able to locate the seventh Righter?"

"We haven't," DiCaprio replied. "Unexplainably, Visera experiences some type of block when it comes to the seventh Righter. She is sure another Righter exists, but she hasn't had a breakthrough yet. We strongly believe this one could be under Jenroe control, or it is even possible that he or she could be one of the Righters that were exiled here to Exilium. That is why we are working so hard to increase literacy here. However, as I said before, we are learning that if some part of gift has not been discovered while the Righter is a child, it may never develop. I am baffled that among the hundreds of marks that we have encountered not a single individual has displayed the gifts of a Righter.

"How could that be?" Rowe asked.

"We don't have a full understanding of it yet, Rowe. But

we are working on it. Trust me, if there is a way to train and develop more Righters, we will find it. We will need all the help we can get. It is possible; however, that if the seventh Righter is out there, he or she could be writing our world as we live it now. We pray that is not the case, but until we know for sure, we must be careful. We have lookouts in all the territories." DiCaprio stopped and looked at her intently.

"But what we need right now, Rowe, is for you to be on board. What do you say?"

Rowe paused and deeply contemplated his words.

"I need to see my father," she abruptly cried out. "I *have* to know that he's okay."

Suddenly, there was a familiar voice behind her.

"I'm okay, Rowe."

She whirled around. "Dad!" She nearly flung herself in his arms, but Visera, escorting him in, stepped protectively between them. Rowe saw how severely beaten he was. A wave of nausea washed over her, and tears stung her eyes. "Why didn't you fight back, Dad? For God's sake, you're a sixth-degree black belt."

"They would've killed me, Rowe." He smiled tenderly at

her. "I had to stay alive for you."

General Pense, a very large man, slumped to the floor from injury and exhaustion as Rowe and Visera did their best to steady him. Rowe felt something powerful building up inside her . . .

"I'm in!" she said as she turned to DiCaprio. "So, what's this plan you keep talking about, and what's my role in it?"

DiCaprio nodded. A smile crept across his face. "The time has come to right a one-thousand-year wrong. We've assessed your skills from afar. True, you are quite a fighter, young lady, but more so, you are our strongest story writer. Your literary and combat skills are far beyond what any of us are capable of, so we will be depending on you to write this. It's time to write the first battle. And we will call your story, *"The Righting Wars."*

Chapter 15∞
RIGHTER'S BLOCK

The Sparrow home in Imperium was fairly quiet. The dawn of evening had fallen upon the landscape of the territory as Jana and Philmore sat quietly on their back patio by the pool, not uttering a word, each engrossed in their own private thoughts and concerns.

The call for the capture of the Pense family dominated the news. Both Jana and Philmore felt helpless. They worried about the danger that Piper might be in. They also worried about Keelie. It was no secret that if Piper were in any danger, with both Alfred and Maya missing, Keelie would be Piper's first phone call. However, she had not contacted Keelie, as far as they knew, and they had no idea if their daughter, or Maya and Alfred for that matter, were dead or alive.

"Do you think they are okay?" Jana quietly asked,

breaking the silence that stood between them. Philmore paused before letting out a dejected sigh.

"I'm not sure," he replied. "I'm more worried about Keelie. If Piper is in hiding, Keelie could very well be instrumental in helping her escape the administration."

"They would kill her," Jana desperately responded. The same thought had crossed her mind several times, and she, too, was worried about Keelie's safety. She bit her lip as her eyes sought his. "I guess you and I are still connected in more ways than I thought . . . at least when it comes to the kids."

"You think so?" Philmore softly questioned, looking away. "I thought we'd lost that connection years ago when I allowed Piper to be taken away.

"Oh, Phil! There was nothing you could have done to change what happened that night. There was nothing you could have done to change what happened to me! Look at me, Phil."

Philmore slowly looked back at his wife. He was flushed red, and Jana witnessed something she had not witnessed in years. Tears were rolling down his cheeks.

She put her hand softly on his. "I chose to drown my pain in alcohol, Phil. You have done everything in your power to save me from myself, and I have fought you at every turn."

"I should have tried harder!"

"And what more do you think you could have done?"

". . . I . . . I don't know. Maybe . . . be a better husband . . . a better father to Patton and maybe, just maybe, have told Piper the entire truth."

"No, Philmore!" Jana exploded into tears. "That is not your truth to tell. You have been a great father and a great husband. You've stayed with me through the drinking and the depression, never leaving my side. Phil, you have been all that you can be to us, including Piper and Patton. It has been my secret, my drinking, and my awful advice to my daughter to marry into that God-forsaken Jenroe family that has us in this mess. I will *not* allow you to breathe another moment feeling guilt nor spend another day bearing the blame for things that were outside of your control. I want so desperately to fix this, Phil, but I'm so far gone that I don't know where to start. I drink because I'm empty. I'm scared. I'm broken. I just want to be whole again."

Jana Sparrow was a sobbing mess as her husband embraced her. He had not held her so tightly in years. Only moments ago, she felt as if she were falling apart, but Philmore's embrace, if only for that moment, held her together. She had always known he loved her, but in that very moment, she felt it.

"Mom, Dad?" Patton softly called out. They both turned to see him standing next to the French doors of the patio, anxiously ringing his hands.

"Yes, dear?" Jana answered, covertly wiping away her tears.

"The news says Alfred Pense was caught, but he's escaped again. What's going on?"

"We're not sure, son," Philmore replied, waving for him to join them."

Patton walked onto the patio and sunk down on the large sofa. He looked anxiously from one to the other. "Does Keelie know what's going on?"

"I'm sure she does," Jana replied.

"Well, she doesn't need to get involved!" Patton exploded. "I know she loves Piper, but Piper's no longer our problem. She belongs to the Penses now! I wish this would all just go away!"

"Don't say that, Patton!" Jana snapped.

Suddenly, the doorbell rang.

"I'll get that," said Philmore. He slowly adorned them both with a kiss on the forehead. "Don't worry. We'll get through this together."

After a second ring of the doorbell, Jana strained to hear what was going on.

"Philmore Sparrow?"

"Yes," replied Philmore. "How can I help you?"

"We're from the Jenroe administration."

"I know who you are!" Philmore scoffed. "What can I do for you?"

We've been sent here to check your home for possibly harboring Piper Sparrow."

"You've been what?"

Jana sprung to her feet and headed to the front door. Patton followed.

"What's going on?" asked Jana.

"We apologize for disturbing your evening, ma'am," an official continued. "But we have been sent to check your home."

Jana placed her arm on Philmore's shoulder. "It's okay, Phil, let them check."

She turned to the official. "You're welcome to check our home, sir, but Piper terminated us recently. We no longer have any contact with her or the Pense family."

"I understand, ma'am. But we have orders."

Jana and Philmore stepped aside as four men in black militia dress suits entered their home. The men quickly split up.

"You two take the upstairs," one ordered the others.

"I'll take the basement, and you check this floor thoroughly."

The Sparrow family sat powerless as the Jenroe administration invaded their home—once again. Only this time it wasn't the medical mission. It was the Jenroe militia. Jana could sense the fear in Patton. She wrapped her arms around him to console him, but what worried her more was the fury she saw in Philmore's eyes.

"Don't do anything rash, Philmore. This will be over soon."

They waited in silence. Moments later, the men returned.

"We're sorry for the intrusion," said one of the officials, handing Jana a business card. "However, should you hear from Miss Sparrow, would you please give me a call?"

Jana eyed the card. "Wh . . . what is this all about?"

"Miss Sparrow and the Pense family are wanted for first degree sedition."

Jana gasped as the color drained from her face.

"What!" Philmore stared, slack-jawed. "She's a child! There has to be a mistake!"

"No mistake, sir. As I stated, please contact me should you hear from her."

The four men exited the Sparrow home. Philmore collapsed in the recliner, and Jana sobbed.

"Mom, what is the punishment for first degree sedition?" Patton slowly asked.

"It's punishable by death," she whispered.

∞∞∞∞∞∞∞∞∞∞

Rowe was led to a room where she encountered Connor Spalding working away on his computer. Immediately, she was drawn to him. He was a fairly handsome young man with a slender, yet muscular build. She sat down at her desk across from him.

"Hi." She noticed right away he seemed shy. "I'm Rowe."

"I know who you are," Connor responded without looking up from the computer.

"What are you working on?" She got up and walked over to his desk to peer over his shoulder.

"I'm putting together a digital prototype of a militia machine gun. We may need these when we're done. The rays that they shoot are of radium. They'll take the enemy out immediately, and they won't feel any pain."

Rowe whistled. "Wow, that's something. We don't want the Jenroes to get their hands on this . . . or we'll all be dead. Which appears to be their plan, anyway."

Connor shuffled uneasily in his chair. He nodded nervously in agreement. "However," he continued with an air of defensiveness, "they don't have a chance of getting their hands on this or any of our other plans. We are well hidden here, but in all fairness, I can only guess what types of weapons we'll need until you get the story written. Once you write the story and the portal opens for us, then I can prepare the weapons we'll take through it when we go."

Rowe picked up on his abruptness. She took his last statement as a cue that she should be writing, not bothering him.

"Oh . . . um . . . I guess you're right. I'd better get started." As she stood, she gestured toward the computer screen. "By the way, I have a degree in advanced technology. You know I could help with that."

"I don't need any help," Connor snapped. "Just concentrate on the story."

Gauging he was clearly annoyed, Rowe sat back at her desk in silence.

"Your supplies are in the top drawer to your right," Connor said as he continued to stare directly at his computer, avoiding eye contact.

Rowe remained at the desk for an hour. She made no progress. Slowly the paper basin beside her began to fill, as Connor occasionally eyed her from his desk. After hours of complete silence, he finally spoke.

"Are you having writer's block?"

His voice startled her, causing her to jump. She had been nodding in and out of sleep.

"What . . . What did you say?"

"I said, are you having writers block?" Connor condescendingly repeated, raising his voice."

"Well . . . uh, yes!" Rowe defensively replied. She immediately picked up her pen and began writing again. Moments later, completely frustrated, she began crumpling page after page of her story. She got up again and sat next to Connor.

"Can I ask you question?" she asked.

"You just did."

"No, I mean . . . well, you know what I mean."

"Yes, Miss Sparrow, you are welcome to ask me a question." A slight smile crept across his face as he finally made eye contact with her.

Rowe instantly froze. His eyes were a striking blue. But in that second, she remembered Connor's gift of mind reading and she swiftly turned away. Connor's unwillingness to make eye contact with her suddenly made sense. He must have picked up on her frustration and found it quite amusing that she had become somewhat irritated.

"Some people are easier to read and control than others," Connor said, as if to reassure. "You have a strong mind. And don't worry, I won't read your thoughts, and I won't make you do anything you don't want to do."

Rowe shook off her unease. "If we're all righters, then why am I the only one writing the story?"

"Because they say you're the best."

"Well, I don't feel like the best right now. I can't seem to put two sentences together."

"Sometimes," a familiar voice said from behind her, "it's best to write how you're most comfortable writing."

Rowe turned to find DiCaprio standing in the doorway.

"I've come to check on the two of you. I see you've become acquainted."

Rowe rolled her eyes. "Yes, thanks for leaving me in here with good old Connor, the barrel of laughs. I can't get enough of the unending chatter."

"Well, Connor is rather quiet," DiCaprio said with a smile. "He's an introvert at heart, but once he gets to know you, trust me, he'll warm up."

Connor noisily cleared his throat. "I am sitting right here, folks." He continued to stare deeply into the computer screen.

DiCaprio leaned against the edge of Rowe's desk. "When you have written in the past, Rowe, where were you, and what were your surroundings?"

She frowned and thought. "Well, of course I was alone."

"Alone where?"

"In my room."

"Exactly. Connor, would you show our newest member to her room?"

"Sure, I think I'll call it a night, too," Connor said, pushing back his chair. "Follow me."

Connor took Rowe to a hall just outside of their office.

"Your room is the one on the left at the end of the hall. There's a key under the mat for you. Be sure to activate voice recognition as soon as you get in to ensure no one can get into your room. It's a part of our lock down plan should anyone ever infiltrate us."

"Wow," Rowe said, amused, as she stared at the metal name plate of the hall. "We live on Righter's Block? Quite befitting."

She walked two doors down the hall, bent down to retrieve the key, then opened the door. As she stepped inside, she looked over her shoulder to discover Connor staring at her.

"Just making sure you're able to get in," he said nervously.

"I'll be fine," Rowe said with a wink. "I think I'm in friendly territory, and I'm a six-degree black belt."

Connor blushed a brilliant red.

"Well, good night," he said as he rushed into his room.

As the door clicked shut behind her, Rowe suddenly felt lonely. She wanted to see her mother. She was very worried about her. The room was cold and sterile, not much like her room at home, but it did have the privacy she needed, and now she didn't have the distraction of Connor pecking away at his keyboard.

She took a deep breath. Suddenly, her thoughts came into focus. She remembered when she was a child. She had dreamed of the opportunity to one day put a cease to the injustices of the Jenroe regime, and now she had her chance. The memory of the six-year-old version of her story suddenly flooded her mind. She wrote furiously.

Rowe wrote throughout the night, but once the story was complete, she still couldn't sleep. She couldn't get the beautiful images of the old country out of her mind. She wanted to go back into the room with the digital screens and imagine what the United Missions could truly be one day, but wondered if she could even get in. After several minutes of contemplating, she decided to go for it.

The Hall of "Righter's Block" was very quiet, but she noticed a hint of light beaming from under a slight crack at the bottom of Connor's door.

Should I wake him? Rowe thought, but she decided that she could do it all on her own. As she made her way through the confusion of the compound, she remembered the doors were voice recognition. She was relieved to discover that she had already been cleared. Each door leading to the room opened with ease. When she finally reached her destination, the screens were still there some of them floating as if they were awaiting her arrival.

Rowe slowly raised her hand as she attentively filed through each screen. The scenes were completely beautiful. At first, she was in awe, but suddenly the most horrific scene was before her.

"What is this?" Rowe whispered to herself as she stared at the screen in horror. The Captions read "The Great Gathering". Tears streamed down her face as she witnessed militia men slaughtering thousands of people. Screen after screen showed the horror of men, women and children being gathered only to be lead across what appeared to be a desert land and completely annihilated without mercy.

Rowe was mortified as she watched the scenes of militia men smiling and laughing as the horrified victims begged for their lives. Scenes of thousands of emaciated people being thrown into gas chambers and annihilated, bombarded the floating screen. All she could do was turn away as the tears and emotion overwhelmed her.

Suddenly she caught sight of DiCaprio quietly standing behind her.

"There were thousands," she whispered.

"No," DiCaprio quietly replied, "Six million in all were murdered! So now you know why this is so important. Now you must truly understand why we have to do this."

Rowe did not respond. She quietly exited and returned to her room. She suddenly felt ill as the images of the violence swarmed in her head. She thought she would vomit as she found herself on her knees gasping for air beside her bed. For one second, she thought she might pray, but even at such a vulnerable moment, she was unable to give in to her mother's influence. She questioned her mother's faith even more after witnessing the horrific events of the Great Gathering.

"What God would allow that to happen to innocent people?" She cried out, not caring if everyone in the compound heard her as she slowly crawled under her covers.

At some point, in the early morning hours before dawn, she must have drifted off as she cried herself to sleep, but not long after that she was awakened all too soon by DiCaprio knocking at her door.

"Are you joining us for breakfast?"

"Be there in a minute." She groggily whispered, as she simultaneous stretched, feeling stiff, but at the same time trying to alleviate herself of the sinking feeling that the scenes from the great gathering had given her.

"Just follow the signs to the eating hall," DiCaprio said.

Rowe splashed water on her face and smoothed out her shirt she had yet to change. It still reminded her of home. Later she would pick through the new wardrobe they had provided her. She took a cursory look in the mirror and hastily left her room to head down the hallway. As she entered the dining area, she felt all eyes on her. She could tell by the looks of anticipation that everyone was waiting to see if she had completed the story. Jenna Davis, Xander Romanov, and Princley Kerr were all there. She nervously handed over the stack of papers to DiCaprio without saying a word.

DiCaprio looked over the story. Slowly, he began to smile. He looked up.

"Ladies and gentlemen, I now have for you the beginning of the *Righting Wars—The Initiation!*

Chapter 16∞

The Story

Rowe slowly scanned the table. DiCaprio sat at the head with Visera to his right and her dad, who was regaining his strength, to his left. Her eyes stopped on Visera. Her mysterious appearance made it difficult to decipher whether she was Sunz or Metisse, but there was a mystery about her that made Rowe shudder. She noticed there was an empty seat for her, next to her dad and beside Connor, who was chatting with Dr. Dara Cleary across the table. The remainder of those seated at the table were Righters, including Harper Whitson.

As Rowe silently surveyed the group, she recognized each of the Righters from their images she had seen on the screens the previous day. Jenna Davis was a tall, slender girl, a pure Sunz in appearance with skin like caramel and a striking cheekbone structure. Her physique belied a strength that seemed to exude from within. She had the countenance of a warrior, and she was someone Rowe was glad to have on her team.

Xander Romanov was intriguing. He was an obvious Metisse, appearing to have some Asian features that Rowe recognized from the footage she viewed of the Old World. Yet, his light-colored hair was of the Palers, obvious proof that he was a result of the war that had taken place, along with America's ensuing and desperate need to survive by procreation. His thick obscure eyeglasses and excessively geeky mannerisms made him appear quite the nerd, but his talents would be invaluable to the cause. Rowe had written him into her story to do exactly what was needed of him.

Princley Kerr sat to the left of Xander and appeared highly enthusiastic. She, too, was a Metisse, but seemed to have more of the Middle Eastern features of the Old World. Her hair was a raven black that fell over her shoulders like silk. She was beautiful, appearing almost delicate. However, knowing her levitation and flight skills helped Rowe to see her in a different light.

So, this is my team, Rowe thought as she took her seat.

"How's Mom?" Rowe whispered to her dad.

"Your mother is fine. Some of us went out during the

night to check on her and a few of the others."

"Did you tell her I was with you?" Rowe asked.

"Yes, and she's worried senseless. I promised that I would keep you safe."

Rowe smiled slightly. She nervously squeezed his hand.

"Dad, you trained me to be a sixth-degree black belt. I can take care of myself."

"Well, that's to be seen. You've never had to use it in actual combat. However, I'm sure that will be tested soon, if the story you just turned over to DiCaprio is anything like the one you wrote at six years old."

Rowe paused. She knew the stories were almost identical, but this time she knew the players in the story. She knew their talents, their capabilities, and their skills. However, she also knew that her story could control time and the characters it accounted for. Any unsuspected players or deviation from the storyline could lead to a catastrophic outcome and a devastating defeat on their first mission.

"So, what do we do first?" Rowe asked as she turned to DiCaprio, who was engrossed in her story. A hush settled over the room as DiCaprio turned to the last page and finally finished the last line. He looked up from the paper with a smile. It was clear he was pleased with Rowe's story.

"First, we enjoy breakfast," DiCaprio answered, but loud enough to squelch the anticipatory stares of the others. "After breakfast, we will give everyone copies of your story. Visera, please make copies for each operative at this table."

Soon after they began eating, Visera took Rowe's story and exited the room. DiCaprio lowered his voice and continued to address Rowe.

"Did a portal open when you completed the story?"

"Yes, but the better I get at this, the more I can control when and where a portal opens. I closed it off in my quarters last night by simply folding over the paper. I can feel when it opens. It is still closed off."

"Rowe?" Alfred gasped. "You mean to tell me that you have been practicing with this . . . this dangerous . . . thing?"

"Not really, Dad." Rowe was aloof. "Nothing dangerous, only small things, like what's for breakfast or getting my homework done."

Alfred squinted suspiciously. "What about your training? Did you change that?

"*No*, Dad, I promise. I truly earned my levels—every one of them."

Alfred was silent. He took a nervous sip of his coffee. "We'll soon find out," he said under his breath.

Visera returned to the room and began passing out copies of the story.

"Study these," DiCaprio ordered. "Learn your role. Then destroy them. This is the first of three stages, and we should have it completed within the month. Rowe will be working on Stage II and III in the meantime. Each stage will largely depend on the success of the previous stage. We must stay on course and stick to the story for the ending to play itself out. However, we must be keenly aware that if any of us deviate from the storyline in any way, it could affect all of us—and some of us may not survive."

The room was silent.

Jenna Davis shifted uncomfortably in her seat and glared at Princely. "I'm not so sure everyone at this table can be trusted. How do we know we haven't already been infiltrated?"

"Jenna, we don't need that negativity," Harper snapped.

"No, Harper," Connor interrupted. "She could have a point. Xander and Princley are Christian and from Metisse. They are definitely not as oppressed as those of us who come from Righting and other territories."

Connor glared at them. "So, why *are* you here?"

Xander and Princley traded glances, incensed.

"We lose our family members, too," Xander retaliated, slamming his fist on the table. "Let's not forget, many in our group must hide our individual faiths. We must pretend to be of another heritage in order to survive. Yes, we all look similar. But look at us! We are made of blacks, whites, Hispanics, Persians, Indians, and we must all claim the race of Metisse. We are forced to practice the government's mandated religion. Our identities were stolen from us by the Jenroe administration. If that's not oppression, then what is?"

"All of us saw the films," Princley added, pushing her chair away from the table and standing. "Each of us saw how unified the country was before the election of 2016. That unity was what made the United States of America so great. We want that back just as much as you do. No one wants this more than Xander and I do. We are all in! We won't back down or be pushed out of the movement because of your insecurities, Jenna!"

Rowe sensed an animosity between Jenna and Princley

that seemed to be from an unspoken history.

DiCaprio calmly gestured for Princely to sit down. "Thank you, both of you. I am confident that each of us here can be fully trusted. Remember, Visera is the only one among us with a special gift who does not carry the mark, and she is a mind reader. She has carefully assisted me to vet each of you. With that said, I recommend that each of you head to your quarters or wherever you feel you can study best. We will reconvene at dinnertime and begin planning. In the meantime, Princley, General Pense will be working with you on some self-defense techniques. Rowe, we may need you to spar with her, since you're familiar with your story. I am sure you won't need to study."

Rowe glanced at Princely, and she smiled back. She didn't think Princley looked like much of a fighter, but her gift of levitation and flight definitely came in handy in constructing the story.

DiCaprio's voice interrupted her thoughts. "As for the rest of you, before we reconvene at dinner, we will also meet this afternoon to start practicing your less-developed talents."

Everyone dispersed throughout the underground compound. Rowe needed to retrieve more writing supplies, so she returned to the office where she and Connor worked. This time the other desks were occupied by the Righters, now reading Rowe's story intently.

Harper Whitson was there as well, and memories flooded back of her old job at the press office with Harper at the helm. Unlike the Righters, his office was closed off and separate from their desks, but she could clearly see him through the glass windows that separated the rooms. His desk was an absolute mess. Back at the paper, his immaculate assistant, Avery Jones, kept him organized. Here, Rowe could clearly see that he was barely functioning without her, but diligently studying his part in the story.

As Rowe wondered what to do next, she meandered over to Conner and peered over his shoulder. "What are you working on? Shouldn't you be studying my story?"

Connor sighed, agitated. "Well, you modified the capabilities of my radium guns in the story. I'm changing the specifications for the prototypes. My guns incinerate their targets but leave behind deposits. The guns in your story completely dissipate the target. No deposits or trace of matter can be found. Unfortunately, that is not an easy feat as matter can be transformed . . ."

". . . but can't be created or destroyed," they both said in unison.

"So, you do remember sixth grade physical science, I see," Connor mocked.

Rowe rolled her eyes. "Touché. I guess I'll leave you to your genius."

"I would appreciate that."

Rowe returned to her room. There wasn't much she could do now but wait on the others to finish studying the first story. As she lay on her bed, staring at the ceiling, her thoughts drifted to her mother and Keelie. She didn't know how to feel about Keelie giving birth to a Jenroe. She felt somewhat betrayed. The only thing that gave her solace was Dara assuring her that Keelie tried to prevent it.

Unfortunately, the Jenroes now knew of Keelie's betrayal. Rowe was worried for her safety. Contacting her was not an option at this point, and Keelie would never come to Exilium. Rowe knew she had to find a way to reach her.

Rowe's eyes were heavy. Exhaustion had finally caught up with her, and soon she drifted off. She was in a deep, restful sleep, when DiCaprio tapped on her door at noon.

"It's time to learn what you're really capable of, Rowe."

Chapter 17∞

The Coliseum

Rowe and DiCaprio entered the state-of-the-art arena to find Alfred Pense and the Righters awaiting their arrival.

"Wow!" Rowe marveled as she gazed around the enormous building. "This place is amazing."

DiCaprio smiled proudly. "Thank you. I have to admit, my dear, it was once just a ruin. A great deal of hard work went into refurbishing this. It was what the old Americans called an arena or a coliseum. After the destruction of the United States over a thousand years ago, much of the infrastructure was destroyed. This particular structure was originally built underground. After the war, it was believed to have been destroyed, but we unearthed it while secretly tunneling to build the underground passage. Coincidentally, it became a part of the building plans."

Rowe nodded, then put on an animated impersonation of Maya. "Well, as my mom would say, the Lord works in mysterious ways."

"Yes, she would," Alfred agreed, shaking his head in amusement. "You're pretty good at that but stop making fun of your mom. She means well and tries to teach you right."

"So, this place is a rather nice touch," Rowe said to DiCaprio. She wasn't in the mood to argue with her dad on the subject of Maya and her religious rants.

"Well, it's just what we need for our mission," DiCaprio said. Abruptly, he clapped twice. "Ok, Righters, everyone to the center."

At the center of the enormous building were circular steps leading to a round platform. The Righters stood in linear formation.

"Hello, Righters," DiCaprio continued. "Today new abilities will be awakened. Prepare to learn skills that will push you beyond what you've fathomed. Each of you has perfected at least one of your natural gifts. However, you have dormant skills. I'll use myself to demonstrate one of them. The first clue that I possessed amazing capabilities was my ability to morph. As Righters, we all have this ability. Please, allow me to demonstrate."

DiCaprio stood in a solid stance, his feet spread apart. Suddenly, his brown eyes turned a piercing green. Rowe and the others drew back in horror as the immediate cracking of bones and stretching of skin turned the handsome young man into a grotesque, twisted version of a wild animal they could not yet identify.

DiCaprio let out a blood curdling sound, more like a howl than a scream. The others, along with Alfred, were chilled to the bone. They stared into the penetrating green eyes of the vicious wolf-like creature while it encircled them like trapped prey. Their silence magnified the terror as echoes of panicked breathing and a low, sinister growl filled the arena. As fast as he had transformed himself into the beast, a normal DiCaprio stood facing them once again. he seemed amused with their sighs of relief.

"How did you do that?" Rowe burst out.

"It takes practice. I do not expect any of you to perfect this overnight. However, your ability to morph—or what you choose to morph into—is up to you. I assure you that you will discover your beast of preference."

Princely crinkled her nose. "I don't think I can do that. It's . . . it's gross!"

"Well then, find something that you can live with," DiCaprio said dryly. "You all need to realize that your ability to master these skills is dire to your survival. We're not playing games here. We are about to begin a revolution against some of the most ruthless leaders in the history of this country. You have been given the tools to win this war. If you fail to use them, trust me, you will die! Think about this. When you're ready, we will try again."

DiCaprio began to exit off the platform.

"Wait!" Rowe blurted out. "I'll do it! How do I do it?"

DiCaprio turned and smiled. "Now that's what I'm talking about. Piper Sparrow, what is your beast of choice?"

Rowe's mind raced. "Eagle!"

"Eagle, is it? Good choice. Are you ready?"

"I . . . I guess." Rowe didn't know where to begin. She waited on DiCaprio's cue. "What do I do?"

"You begin, my dear, by relaxing."

Rowe took a deep breath. She tried to shake off her fear,

but the unnerving image of DiCaprio's transformation plagued her mind.

"Now, close your eyes," DiCaprio spoke quietly, placing his hands on Rowe's shoulders from behind.

Rowe closed her eyes. For the first time in a long time, she was truly nervous. Discovering her writing abilities as a child had been unsettling enough. But changing form? This was beyond what she could imagine. She wasn't sure if she could pull it off.

She was aware of DiCaprio's breath on her neck. "What do you see in your mind's eye?" he whispered in Rowe's ear.

"I see you changing into that thing . . ."

"Don't think about me. Concentrate! Keep your eyes closed, relax, and stay focused.

Cringing, Rowe squeezed her eyes shut. "You don't have to yell," she said under her breath.

DiCaprio's hands loosened on her shoulders. "Relax, Miss Sparrow. Imagine your wings. Imagine your beak. Imagine that your arms are transforming into the glorious wings of an eagle. Allow them to relax and flow."

Rowe took long, deep breaths. She concentrated hard.

She focused on DiCaprio's voice and imagined an eagle soaring through the sky . . .

"What are you seeing now?' DiCaprio asked.

"I see the sky."

"What do you feel?"

"I . . . I feel normal."

"Feel yourself changing . . . Feel the earth flow from beneath you."

Rowe focused hard, but her heart continued to race. Nothing happened. She could still feel her arms. They were not transforming into the wings that she was imagining them to become.

"I can't do this," she finally gasped.

"Yes, you can. You have to!" demanded DiCaprio.

Rowe fought back tears.

"Wait a minute, DiCaprio," Alfred's stern voice broke in. "Aren't you being a little hard on her? She's never done this before. Take it easy."

Rowe regained concentration. Hearing her dad's voice and remembering what he endured gave her new determination. She had to do it. She wasn't going to fail.

DiCaprio continued, "Concentrate, Rowe! Imagine your wings. Imagine soaring above us all. You decide the eagle that you become. Do it! Do it, Piper Sparrow! You are an eagle. Say it!"

"I am an Eagle," Rowe whispered.

"Say it again!" DiCaprio demanded.

"I am an eagle."

"Keep saying it! Over and over! Keep saying it."

"I am an eagle," Rowe repeated, raising her voice.

"Louder!" DiCaprio urged. "Say it loud! Scream it out! Believe it, Piper Sparrow! You must believe it."

Rowe tried as hard as she could, but she still didn't feel anything happening. But soon a silence settled over the room. She kept her eyes closed.

"That's it," said DiCaprio.

"Oh, my God Rowe!" Princely whispered.

Rowe felt a tingling travel through her. With her eyes still closed, she focused on the strength and power now surging through her.

"Do you feel your arms?" DiCaprio asked quietly.

"Yes," Rowe whispered.

They felt heavy and light at the same time. Then the rest of her body began to feel like her arms. She was beginning to feel as if she could float away."

"Concentrate, Rowe!"

She could hear a sense of triumph in DiCaprio's words. "Concentrate," DiCaprio whispered again. "Imagine the sky. Feel yourself soar. Now open your eyes and concentrate!"

Slowly, Rowe began to open her eyes. Something was different. Her eyesight was magnified. Small details, down to the tiniest cracks and crevices in the walls of the room, were clearly visible. She knew the eyesight of an eagle was flawless, greater than three times that of human vision. The sensory overload she felt was overwhelming. She felt as if she needed to escape. DiCaprio's voice, which had now returned to a whisper, oddly seemed louder, yet at the same time, more distant.

"Now, soar!" DiCaprio echoed in her ear.

Still confused, she peeked at her arms. Glorious and expansive wings shimmered in the light of the stadium. Certainly, she wasn't really looking at herself, she thought. Yet, the growing sense that this was indeed her body, and that she was in complete control, spread through her.

"Soar! Rowe, soar!" DiCaprio's voice echoed again. Before she knew it, she swiftly rose toward the light. With ease and agility, as if in a dream, she glided and soared around the arena in full flight.

It took a minute for her to realize that she was truly in

full eagle form, soaring above everyone in the building. It wasn't until she saw Alfred and his look of wonder that she began to really believe. As she soared, she stared at her wings, the heavy feathers, and the talons. Most of all, she couldn't believe how clearly, she saw even the tiniest detail as she swooped above them.

Rapidly, she began to tire. The expansive wings felt heavy. She knew she needed to return to where the others were just beneath her. Slowly, she glided back in with a swoop, landing squarely in the center of the platform. Her arms felt lighter after landing. The sensory overload that she felt seconds earlier subsided. However, the more it dissipated, the more drained she felt and the more grounded and confined to gravity she became.

Overwhelmed with a sense of vertigo, she couldn't decipher whether she had truly landed on the platform or whether she was still in full flight. As the seconds passed, and the spinning of the room ceased, Rowe came to her senses to find herself half kneeling on the platform. She looked up. All eyes were on her. Her gaze locked on her dad's. His eyes were moist and filled with pride.

DiCaprio held out his hand and helped Rowe up.

"Wow," Rowe managed to say. Her chest rose and fell with rapid breaths. "I'm completely exhausted."

"The more you do it, the easier it gets," DiCaprio said. He turned to the others. "Each of you will practice the skill of morphing. Now, there is more."

He pointed to Connor. "Demonstrate."

Connor whipped his head around to glare at Xander Romanov. Rowe covered her mouth with her hand. Conner bore down on Xander with a stare that made him unable to move a muscle. Several gasped as, without warning, Xander turned around and viciously locked his fingers around the

delicate neck of Princley. Caught off guard, Princley switched into full defense mode, demonstrating her skill of levitation and flight. She swiftly soared into the dark depths of the arena ceiling taking Xander with her as she fought to break his grasp.

Rowe watched in horror as Princely struggled for air above

her, digging her fingers into Xander's arms to free herself from his death grip. Princely finally returned to the platform at the mercy of Connor, the only one who could break the mind control. Connor blinked, releasing his hold on Xander.

"Oh my God, Princley, I'm so sorry!" Xander pleaded as he quickly released his grip on her wind pipe.

"You!" Xander yelled in a rage as he charged toward Connor. Rays of fire exploded from his hands.

"I would not do that if I were you," Connor warned. "You love her, don't you? You've loved her since you first laid

eyes on her. Do I need to keep on talking, or do you want to calm down?"

As if nothing had happened, DiCaprio turned to Rowe. "Later, you will be sparing with Princley. She needs a lot of work."

Gauging by the murmurings, Rowe could tell no one was ready to move on, especially Princely who stared at Conner with narrowed eyes.

"Why did you do that?" Princely screamed. "I could have killed him if he had let go up there."

"That's enough, all of you!" snapped DiCaprio. "This was for your benefit. Connor has simply demonstrated how to control the mind and read it. Princely has demonstrated levitation and fight. And in an attempt to defend himself, Xander has demonstrated how to create fire. Each of you possesses these same abilities, but you will not, nor will you

ever, use them on one another. If you want to be angry at someone, then be angry with me. Connor did not want to demonstrate. He simply obeyed. Now, for our last skill. Release the beast, General Pense.

Suddenly, the loud sound of an opening cell door startled everyone. The enormity of the building magnified the growl of an approaching animal, yet none of the Righters could tell what direction the menacing growl came from. As the rest stood in defensive mode, Jenna Davis stepped out to the front.

Slowly, she canvassed her surroundings, very much aware that a beast of some sort could appear at any moment. As her breathing began to relax, the enormous beast reared its head with a loud roar, approaching Jenna from behind.

"Jenna, look out!" Rowe screamed.

Jenna abruptly turned with a swift and skilled tumble,

just in time to escape the attack of a lion-like beast. The creature crouched and slowly approached Jenna again, flashing his incisors as they oozed saliva.

"Hold on, boy," Jenna whispered. "Calm down." They encircled one another while facing off. The beast suddenly appeared confused. As its anger began to wane, Jenna moved in closer toward the animal.

"Oh my!" Princley whispered with widened eyes as Jenna began to stroke the mane of the enormous beast.

"There you go, boy," Jenna softly spoke as she nestled in closer.

Within seconds, no longer were they in the presence of a large angry beast. They were witnessing the animal purr like a house cat as Jenna affectionately stroked his back.

DiCaprio began to applaud. ". . . And that, my fearless Righters, is how you communicate with beasts. She turned to face it, and the animal calmly walked away. Seconds later, the closing of the cell could be heard. Everyone in the room let out a simultaneous sigh.

"Wow, Jenna, that was awesome!" said Rowe.

"Oh, it gets better," said Jenna. "Wait until you need rain, wind, or thunder."

"You can all perform these skills," said DiCaprio, "but as

I said, it will take time. I need each of you to practice diligently. When you are attempting new skills, always be sure you are with the person who has mastery of it until you feel confident with your ability. As we all know, Rowe is our best story writer and has achieved the highest level in militia defense. I am confident in each of you, especially knowing your impressive defense abilities will soon be combined with new skills. So, I recommend that each of you take the time now to pair up and begin practicing. Unfortunately, Princley, you are my exception. Rowe, I need you to spar with Princley, and assist her with her combat skills. She needs a lot of work."

"But what if I can't have her ready in time for the initiation?"

"Well then, it's possible that she won't survive," said DiCaprio flatly.

"What do you mean she won't survive?" said Rowe. "I wrote the story. I decide the outcome!"

DiCaprio clenched his jaw. "Yes, you do, but this is not a game, and you need to understand the limits of your power. If one thing, and I mean absolutely one thing goes wrong or veers off course from how you actually wrote it—we could all die!

Chapter 18∞
Order of Execution

The House of Missions was in an uproar. Dr. Dara Cleary had been added to the growing list of fugitives wanted for first-degree sedition and treason. Keelie was worried sick about Rowe, but something in her heart told her that she was okay. Jefferson, however, was another matter. He had been oddly distant. Recently, he treated her more like an incubator for their child than his wife. He was secretive and no longer sharing with her the details of his meetings with Jeremy and Jackson.

After staying in her room all morning, she felt the walls were closing in on her. She decided that a noon snack in the residence hall would be good for both her and the baby. As she approached the Oval Office, she paused at the sounds of an intense disagreement. She edged closer to the door and heard Jackson's voice raging.

"Alfred and the girl must die!"

"I agree," said a raspy, sinister voice. Keelie recognized it as Patsy Hilleary's. "We can take no chances."

"Not so fast," she heard Jefferson plead. "They're part of my wife's family. Couldn't we just send them to Exilium? Do we have to kill them?"

"Of Course, they must die!" Jackson stormed. "They're traitors!"

Keelie had not heard a peep out of Jeremy, but suddenly his cold voice sent chills up and down her spine.

"I say we find out first who the Righter is. We aren't sure who helped the Penses escape, and the wife knows nothing. We have already interrogated her."

"But we checked Pense thoroughly. It has to be the girl," Jackson insisted.

"It very well may be true that the girl is a Righter," said President Jenroe, "but we must be sure.

"May we discuss this later?" Jefferson asked, lowering his voice. "I'm not comfortable discussing these details with Keelie in the house."

After an awkward pause, she could hear what sounded like

papers shuffling.

"Yes, Jefferson," the president finally responded. "By all means, go spend the day with your lovely wife. Take her somewhere nice. I will fill you in on the details of this meeting later."

"Thank you, Father," said Jefferson. "I think . . . well, I think Keelie could use a day out. She's been really stressed over this entire situation."

"Well, you be sure to alleviate her of that stress," Jenroe said flatly. "I can't have these Sunzes affecting the health of an unborn Jenroe."

Keelie jumped at the sound of the door handle turning. She quickly hid behind one of the columns, then watched as her husband headed toward their bedroom. Keelie felt the color drain from her at Jeremy's words as the door of the oval office clicked shut . . .

"Kill them all. My son is a bit naïve when it comes to that wife of his. If we start with Maya Pense, we may be able to pull the other two out of hiding. Do it and do it now!"

∞∞∞∞∞∞∞∞∞∞

Rowe sensed Princley was nervous. As they sparred, she

tried her best to take it easy on her.

"Good job, Princley," Rowe cheered her on. "Now, as you complete your Dollyo-chagi, just make sure you use the instep of your foot. And look, you're not turning your body far enough. Keep your body at a 45-degree angle. Like this." Rowe demonstrated a perfect round house kick.

"Once you strike the enemy, be prepared for him to come back with something more than what you just delivered. With your levitation skills, you have the element of surprise on your side. Combine the two, Princley, and your first-degree black belt suddenly seems more like a sixth-degree. Now show me what you've got . . ."

Princley nervously took her stance to demonstrate the Dollyo-chagi for her, but then she paused.

"Are you going to move?" Princley asked in a shaky voice.

"No," Rowe replied without flinching. "Show me what you got."

Securing her stance once again, Princley went into a perfect round house kick, knocking Rowe off of her feet. Alfred and DiCaprio were stunned as Rowe yelped in pain. Then instinct kicked in. Rowe immediately came back at Princley with an Ahp-chagi frontal kick.

Surprising everyone, Princley soared through the air into immediate levitation, completing two flips and landing solidly on her feet.

Rowe broke into a smile! "Now *that* is what I'm talking about. I think my work is done here!"

Alfred and DiCaprio slowly clapped. Rowe had been able to do more with Princley in less than an hour than they had accomplished all morning. Rowe grabbed her towel and headed to the water fountain for a drink.

"Hey Rowe," Princley called out, jogging to catch up. "Thanks."

"Oh, no problem," Rowe responded between sips.

"You left the arena so fast, I didn't think I would catch you. I hope I didn't kick you too hard."

"Princley," Rowe replied matter-of-factly, pointing to Alfred who was in deep conversation with DiCaprio, "do you see that man over there? He trained me, and he took no mercy. His kicks were a lot more painful than yours. You just make sure you use your levitation and flight to your advantage. If you allow your opponent to get the upper hand, they could crush you, like Xander almost did. Strike and get out of their reach. That will be to your advantage."

Rowe wiped her face with the towel, then stared into space.

"You seem a little distracted," said Princley. "Are you worried about the plan?"

"No," said Rowe. "I'm just worried about my sister. I'm not sure what the Jenroes have planned for her, or if they even have plans at all. I can't make contact with her from here, but I have to find a way."

Princely frowned. "I think I know someone who may be able to help you. Have you ever heard of Sister Janeth Anderson?

"No," replied Rowe. "Who is she?"

"She's the head of the volunteer medical mission. They travel through all the territories providing medical care to those who can't afford it. She goes into Imperium once a week to get supplies from the Droite Medical Mission. She's a sub-operative under this plan as well. Her job is to bring information from the outside back to DiCaprio. Her headquarters are just above us here in Exilium. Maybe she could set something up with your sister or at the least get a message to her."

Do you think the sister can be trusted?" Rowe asked.

Princely laughed. "She's a nun, Rowe. I would hope so. I will call her. She has full clearance to get into this compound. She may be able to come by at some point today."

"Would you really do that?" Rowe eagerly asked.

Princely smiled. "Are you kidding me? You just taught me moves that I didn't feel I was capable of. I think I want to keep you as a friend."

Rowe laughed and pumped a fist. She glanced at DiCaprio and Alfred who were across the gymnasium still in intense discussion. "Well, Princely, until we know something for sure, could we just keep this between us? I . . . I just don't want to worry my dad."

Princley agreed with a bit of apprehension. "Yes, sure. I'll put in a call to Sister Janeth now."

"Good," said Rowe. "I'm going to take a shower."

As Rowe walked away, she looked back to see Princley lingering. She had to trust that she wouldn't inform DiCaprio or her dad.

Chapter 19∞
Deception

Keelie panicked and rushed into the kitchen. She couldn't let Jefferson know that she had just eaves dropped on their meeting, nor did she trust him enough to tell him the order she had just overheard his father giving. She cringed as the man's cold words continued to plague her. How could this vile man dare to take the innocent lives of the Pense family as well as her sister?

As she sat down on the kitchen chair and rubbed the nape of her neck, she felt a soft touch on her shoulders that made her jump.

"Oh my God, Jefferson, don't do that." Her husband looked at her quizzically, caught off guard by her reaction.

"Hold on, Keelie," he softly spoke as he began to gently massage her. "What's going on with you? You know I would never hurt you . . . don't you?"

Keelie felt apprehensive. "Of course, I know that, Jefferson. I'm just worried about Piper. That's all."

"Don't worry, Keelie. The worst that can happen is that she is captured, and my father sends her to Exilium. She will still be okay."

Keelie sensed his uncertainty. She pulled away and started to cry.

"Look, Keelie, if it makes you feel better, I'll try to get him to be lenient. But we have a child to think about now. You can't allow this stress to affect you like this."

Keelie's phone rang, and she fumbled to pick it up.

"Sister Janeth, why yes, this is Keelie Jenroe. Yes, yes, okay. I can get those supplies for you. Yes, I will be there."

Jefferson frowned.

"Why is Sister Janeth calling you today? Supply pickups are not until next week, and you shouldn't be handling that."

"There's been an emergency in Exilium. She's calling me because this is not a normal day. She's done this before, Jefferson."

"Well, why did you agree to go to her? Exilium is too far

for you to be driving alone, Keelie. I won't allow it."

She stiffened at his tone. "I am not your property! I will go to Sister Janeth, as I have a thousand times before. I will be fine, and you will not stop me!" Keelie's eyes brimmed with tears, but she knew if Jefferson realized how upset she was, it would be even more difficult to leave. She looked away and fidgeted with her wedding ring. "You may not care about the people there. But they are human beings, and I will not contribute to their suffering."

"Well then, I will come with you!" Jefferson demanded.

She stood up and pointed a finger at him.

"No, you will not! I . . . I need to clear my head. I miss my sister. We both know how you feel about her. My best friend and my sister are gone, Jefferson, both at the hands of this administration. I have a hard time crying around you about it, being that you support it."

"Dara gave you birth control, for God sake!" Jefferson yelled.

"So, you knew?" Keelie's face was flushed with anger. "You were in on it, weren't you? You're the reason that I'm going through this! How could you hurt her, Jefferson?"

"Keelie?" His pleading eyes pierced hers. "Do you really believe that I would actually hurt Dara or anyone you love? I was just angry when my father told me about the birth control."

"Your *father*?" Keelie yelled. "How...?"

Jefferson took a deep breath and released a sigh of exacerbation. "He ordered you to be surveilled, Keelie. I didn't find out about the birth control until my father informed me. And yes, Keelie, I was angry!"

"She's innocent," Keelie sobbed. She only gave it to me because I asked for it. I couldn't bear the thought of being forced to sign that paper. I have been angry at my mother all of my life for committing the same act, and now I find myself in that same position. I feel like such a hypocrite!"

"I know, Keelie. I know it hurts, but . . . if . . . if she would have given those pills to you just a month later, we might not ever have been able to have children. Do you understand, Keelie?"

She narrowed her eyes and slowly backed away. "What are you saying, Jefferson?" she whispered in horror. "Exactly what would have been different a month later? Is the administration tampering with the birth control?"

Jefferson was silent.

"Answer me, Jefferson! Are you sterilizing people with the birth control?" She wrapped her arms around her stomach. "Oh my God. I think I'm going to be sick."

Jefferson took her hands in his. She flinched as his hands were clammy.

"Listen to me, Keelie," he begged. "The mandate for illegal birth control in Imperium was passed over a year ago. There will be no more delivered to the Medical Missions here. It will only go to the other three territories. It won't affect us."

"Oh my God, Jefferson, you're all sick . . .What have I done? Why the hell did I marry you?" Keelie grabbed her purse and her keys and stormed through the halls of the House of Missions. She could still hear his voice as she slammed the car door and sped out of the driveway.

"Keelie . . . Keelie . . . I can't lose you, Keelie!"

∞∞∞∞∞∞∞∞∞∞

President Jeremy Jenroe pressed his lips together tightly. He slowly nodded. The surveillance camera that fed into the Oval Office showed Jefferson pulling himself up off the steps. It showed him walking back inside the House of Missions and pausing in front of the supplies—the medical supplies that Keelie had left behind. The president twisted in his leather chair to face the two officers from the Jenroe militia and his brother, Jackson Jenroe, as they awaited his orders.

"It appears my lovely daughter-in-law is a traitor. Follow her!"

∞∞∞∞∞∞∞∞∞∞

Keelie stepped on the gas. She waited until she was far enough beyond the reach of Imperium before making the call. Her fingers shook as she groped in her purse to pull out her cell. She shouted into it, "Call Sister Janeth." It seemed like it took forever to ring.

"Sister Janeth, this is Keelie," she sputtered. "Fine, thank you. Yes, yes, that's perfect. I'll meet you at the designated spot, but I desperately need you to get a message to Maya Pense. Yes, sister Janeth. She's with you? Great. Please let her know she's in danger, grave danger. President Jenroe is planning to execute all three of them . . . both the Penses and my sister. Please, Sister Janeth, get them to safety now, before it's too late."

∞∞∞∞∞∞∞∞∞∞

Rowe heard a tap at the door. Thank goodness, she thought. The underground passage had been far too quiet and uneventful for her. All the other Righters had been busy studying the story and putting together plans for their mission. As she opened the door, her dad stood there with arms folded, eyeing her with an air of disappointment.

"Yes, Dad?"

"Young lady, there is someone here to see you. Is there anything you would like to share with us?"

Rowe opened the door further to reveal an incensed DiCaprio in a wide stance.

"Who's here to see me?" she asked. Her excitement overrode any dread of any possible disciplinary action. She wondered if it was Keelie or Sister Janeth.

"It's Sister Janeth," Alfred suspiciously replied. "Why would you request a meeting with her?"

"Where is she?" Rowe asked, looking down the hall and ignoring them.

DiCaprio slammed his fist against the wall. "I knew this was a mistake. Rowe, do you know how dangerous this is?"

"Well, Princley assured me that Sister Janeth could be trusted, and I only wanted to get a message to Keelie."

"Yes," said Alfred. "We trust Sister Janeth, but can *Keelie* be trusted?"

"Yes, she most definitely can," said a familiar voice.

They turned to see Maya Pense walking down the hall of the compound with Sister Janeth. Rowe froze, wide-eyed.

"Is that really you, Mom?" she gasped.

"Yes, sweetie it's me." Maya said as she rushed to embrace her daughter.

"Alfred," said Maya, looking up but not letting go of Rowe, "you need to know that Keelie sent word through Sister Janeth. Unfortunately, an order has been made by Jenroe to kill both you and me . . . and Rowe. Janeth was able to get me out just in time. We could hear them entering as we took the hidden entrance into the passage. We're not safe out there, Alfred. If it were not for Rowe and Princley getting in touch with Sister Janeth, I would be dead now."

Alfred clenched his jaw. "So, where's Keelie?"

"She's headed to the orphanage. She was sure she was being followed by militia men. She said she'd call once she lost the militia men in Exilium, and it was safe to speak with Rowe."

"Oh no, Maya!" Alfred said. "We can't put Rowe in that kind of danger."

"Alfred, we are already in danger!" snapped Maya. "It can't get much worse. Rowe will be fine. It's Keelie I'm worried about. She has to go back to Imperium alone."

A tense silence was interrupted by the buzz of Sister Janeth's cell. "Yes, Keelie, we're still awaiting your arrival." She turned to Rowe. "Your sister will be arriving soon... It's now or never."

"You stay here," DiCaprio said, pointing to Maya. He took two steps backward and morphed into an exact likeness of Maya.

Maya gasped.

"Should something happen, or should they recognize Rowe, they will end up with me and not you, Maya," DiCaprio said. "Rowe and I have a better chance of escaping than the two of you together."

∞∞∞∞∞∞∞∞∞∞

As Keelie crossed the border into Exilium, she found herself in a downpour. She struggled to see through the pounding rain. Crashes of thunder and flashes of lightning decorated the sky, generating an extra level of anxiety. The lightning was not the only culprit of discomfort. She looked in the rearview mirror.

The car was still following closely. It had been behind her for several miles. As she entered the city, it turned off abruptly. She breathed a sigh of relief. She tried to focus on other things. What would happen to Rowe, Maya, and Alfred? What were her feelings toward Jefferson?

She glanced in the rearview mirror. The vehicle was there again. Someone was watching her. She had to be careful. Luckily the car continued to drive past as she pulled into the orphanage.

She parked, locked the car, and walked quickly to the door, convincing herself that she was just jumpy. Once safely inside the orphanage, she was led directly to Rowe, and they embraced with all their might. They held on to each other for several minutes. As the tears flowed between the two of them, everyone stared in awe. How could two biological sisters of the same mother and father look so different? How could they be so separated in their lives? How could they be so divided by society, yet hold equal love in their hearts for humanity and each other?

"Keelie, I just had to speak with you," said Rowe. "I have to tell you everything."

"Okay, Piper," Keelie replied, looking around nervously. "But I think I am being followed. We have to be careful."

At that, DiCaprio, still disguised as Maya, slipped out to check the perimeter of the building and returned to inform, "It's looks like you are. They're parked down from the orphanage."

"Yes," said Keelie, with a dismissive wave of her hand. "They were aware that I was coming here, so they're probably not too suspicious now. They probably thought they were going to catch me going somewhere else."

She tried to believe this, but her heart pounded in her chest.

She smiled and looked at Rowe.

"At least Exilium is the last place they would expect Rowe to be hiding. Go on, Rowe. Tell me what you need to. I don't have much time."

Rowe went on to share with Keelie about her mark and what it meant. She explained how she discovered her talent as a child and how the Penses had kept her safe all these years.

"I changed the termination papers, Keelie. I never added your name to the list, and I knew that either Jefferson or President Jenroe were responsible for you being on the list. I knew I was taking a chance, but I couldn't bear the thought of never seeing you again. So, I wrote the story and deleted your name from the list, and that is how your name was removed. I had no idea that it would lead to all of this."

Keelie embraced Rowe again.

"Oh, my defiant little sister, what are we going to do with you?" She held her at arm's length and smiled at her.

"We're going to keep her safe," said Sister Janeth. "That's what we're going to do."

"We're working on a plan," said Rowe. "We're going to dismantle the missions. I'm going to use my talent to do it."

The color drained from Keelie's face. "Rowe, you can't say things like that! That's first-degree sedition. You could be killed for that."

"Keelie, they've already given the order to kill me, and I haven't committed any crimes yet. Don't worry, I've written the story so that you're safe during the revolt. I'll be okay, too. But before then, we need to be careful. Do your best to get along with the Jenroes. I'm not sure what they will do to you if they find out about our meeting tonight. I will be okay, Keelie, but I'm afraid for you."

"Don't worry, Rowe, Jefferson loves me. He won't allow them to harm me."

Rowe could only stare at Keelie. *Was she naïve? How could her sister who was so intelligent, beautiful, and filled with so much goodness, put so much faith in such an evil family?* But she had to trust her sister's judgement.

"Well, if you say so," Rowe said. "Just be careful."

"It's time to go now, Rowe," said Sister Janeth.

Keelie grabbed Rowe's hand. "Oh, one more thing. You have to find a way to warn the women of the territories to stop all use of birth control. They are sterilizing them."

Rowe looked to Sister Janeth in horror.

"Oh my, I delivered a batch to Metisse and Righting!" said Sister Janeth. "This is against all that is holy! Father God, help us. DiCaprio, can you warn the people of Metisse and Righting against the sterilization?"

DiCaprio, in the form of Maya, gave sister Janeth a nod and swiftly escorted Rowe back to the secret entrance of the underground passage.

"You need to get busy," he told Rowe, once they had safely re-entered the compound. "We have to change the story and add the warning about the sterilization."

"I will," Rowe said, "but they're going to know Keelie told

us. I'm really worried about her."

"That's Keelie's problem," DiCaprio said coldly. "She can't be on both sides of the fence. Either she's with us or against us. And the same goes for you. She seems to believe that the Jenroes would never turn on her, and in her state right now, she's probably right, but God help her after she gives birth. They will have no more use for her. That's when you should worry."

Chapter 20∞
The Pursuit

Keelie waved goodbye to Sister Janeth. She had been thankful for her escort to the car. Sister Janeth smiled and turned to walk back into the building. As Keelie started the car and headed toward Imperium, she let out a sigh of relief. Not only had the storm subsided, but, more importantly, she felt as if a load had been lifted off of her shoulders. Rowe was safe. Alfred and Maya were alive. Now she could go back to Imperium and work on her relationship with Jefferson. She knew he loved her, but even love could only take so much betrayal. How could she continue to look him in the eyes knowing that she was keeping secrets, the kind of secrets that could have grave consequences?

The Jenroes were dangerous. She knew this better than most others, but her first priority had to be Piper's safety. Now that she was sure her sister was safe, she wouldn't have to betray

Jefferson any longer. The only exception was the secret plans that Piper and the others had shared with her. She rested in the fact that Piper had written the story so that she and her baby would be safe. Then it dawned on her. Nothing had been written about Jefferson's safety. A sense of desperation rose in her.

I have to keep Jefferson safe myself then.

Suddenly, car lights blinded her through the rearview mirror. The car was following too closely. Another glance and she realized it was the same car that had followed her to Exilium. DiCaprio had confirmed she was being followed, but they had dismissed it, certain the Jenroe administration was only verifying she was visiting Exilium. Increasingly, she felt a sense of danger.

Why are they still following me? Maybe it's my imagination.

She sped up to take an alternate route off the rales onto the next exit. If she couldn't lose them, she'd at least confirm whether she was being tailed. Just as she navigated onto the exit ramp, the blinding lights made a sharp turn directly behind her. Panic set in. She accelerated. As she reached a main roadway just off the exit ramp, the vehicle, clearly following her, increased its speed. She had to think quickly. In a sudden act of bravery, she sped through the stoplight that had just turned red. Without hesitation, the other vehicle never broke its momentum and came through directly behind her, hurtling into oncoming traffic. The crashing sound and the screeching of tires shook Keelie to her core, causing her to careen off the road onto the median.

Struggling to maintain control of her own car, she chaotically maneuvered back onto the main highway and was forced to brake in order to avoid oncoming traffic. As her car came to a screeching halt, she made direct impact with the steering column. An excruciating pain radiated through her side. Slowly, she pulled to the side of the road to collect herself. She knew she needed to keep going. Someone was having her tailed, someone from the Jenroe administration. She couldn't stop driving . . . she had to keep going. She had to get home. The pain seared through her.

Oh, my God, my baby!

Jefferson would never forgive her for putting their child in danger. She breathed deeply and tried to calm herself. Slowly, she pulled back onto the highway. Within moments, she was back on route, and there was no sign of anyone following her. The sudden ring of her cell startled her. It was Jefferson. She couldn't tell him what had just happened.

"Hello?" Keelie hoped she had masked any hints of pain in her voice.

"Are you on your way back?" asked Jefferson.

She was happy to hear that he didn't sound angry.

"Yes, dear, I'm back in Imperium city limits. I should arrive in about ten minutes."

"Keelie, please don't do that to me again. I was so worried."

"I promise," Keelie replied, "I just have to accept things the way they are."

"Good girl," Jefferson said.

Keelie arrived, once again, to a quiet and dark House of Missions. With no small children in the home, there were no sounds of joy or echoes of laughter. As she entered their bedroom, Jefferson waited on the bed, flipping through the television channels. She could hear the news bulletins as every news and media outlet reported on the hunt for the Penses. She swallowed hard, hoping Jefferson wouldn't pick up on her discomfort. She sat down on the bed and slipped off her shoes. She sucked in her breath in pain.

"Hey, are you okay?" Jefferson asked, bolting upright. "Why are you holding your side? Did something happen? Is the baby okay?"

"Jefferson, I'm fine," she said and sighed. "It's nothing."

"What do you mean it's nothing?" He lifted her shirt. "What is this, Keelie? What happened?"

Keelie was surprised herself. The impact with the steering column had left a significant bruise on her right side.

"Oh…umm…I avoided a little fender bender on my way back, but I'm a great driver, sweetie. It actually looks worse than it really is. I promise, I'll be fine."

"But what about the baby, Keelie? You have to get checked."

"No, Jefferson." She pushed herself up off the bed, suddenly feeling the weight of the pregnancy, and headed to the bathroom. "I'm tired. I won't get checked tonight. It's better for the baby if I rest. I promise I would never put our baby in danger. If I thought for a second that something was wrong, I would be the first to head to the hospital, but I'm fine. I'm tired, and I'm going to get a shower. I'll come to bed in a minute."

Without warning, Jefferson was up and standing in front

of her. His tone changed, and his eyes pierced her with a cold stare she had never seen before.

"So, how's Sister Janeth?" he asked in a deep, unsettling voice.

"She's fine," Keelie said with a furrowed brow. "Why are you asking about her?"

"Oh, just curious, being that you left the supplies. I would think that Sister Janeth was quite disappointed."

Keelie had to think quickly. She had completely forgotten about the supplies when she had stormed out.

"Well . . . I realized that when I arrived, but I had some extra supplies in the trunk of the car. Thankfully, I didn't have to return to Exilium. That time of night, you really would have had to ride with me."

"Oh, I don't think that would have been necessary," said Jefferson, pausing for effect. "I'm sure that your sister would have been quite disappointed if I'd accompanied you to Exilium."

∞∞∞∞∞∞∞∞∞∞

In the dark, early hours of the morning, Patsy Hilleary grabbed her purse off the table. She liked darkness. Though she was blind, one of her many gifts was the ability to see in the dark.

She walked toward the front gate of the House of Missions. The driver sat patiently awaiting her arrival.

"Where to Ms. Hilleary?" he asked, as he opened the car door for her.

"Righting," she ordered.

Chapter 21∞
Phase I - Black out

The orders were to report to the laboratory at 0400. Rowe's alarm clock sounded at 0300. She wanted to be up early. She needed to mentally prepare for the beginning of the plan. She thought through her story. The Initiation would entail distribution of the propaganda in all the territories at once. The Jenroes would be exposed for what they truly were. The warning about the sterilization process had been written in to the story to avoid throwing off the ending of the Initiation or cause unplanned changes.

If the first part of the wars went as planned, Exilium, Righting, and Metisse would no longer be accessible to those in Imperium—they would be locked out. And there would be just enough time to convince everyone in the territories to organize and join the coup. Many enemies would get locked in along with them, including the militia points in each territory and many Palers, but they would have no contact with the leaders of the Jenroe administration of Imperium. This would allow ample time to perform the coup.

Rowe drew in a deep breath. This was it. She opened her door and headed down the long hall to join the others. The corridor seemed strangely quiet. The sound of her steps seemed ironically insignificant to her as they brought her closer and closer to the events designed to instigate the most significant change in the history of the cruel regime they lived under. She stepped into the laboratory where the other Righters had gathered.

Connor Spalding sat in front on his computer. "The holograms are set to go," he told DiCaprio. "They'll appear in the skies of every territory at one time. The Jenroes will have no idea where the signal is coming from."

DiCaprio nodded to acknowledge Rowe, then stood to face them. "Okay, Righters, we're all here. Let's get started. First, what we are about to do could mean death for any one of us if the plan fails. Prepare to fight the battle of your life. Are you willing to die for your country? If not, then now is the time to bail out. Secondly, we need to watch each other's backs. Use every amount of training and power you have. Do you want to dismantle the territories and defeat the Jenroe administration?"

He paused to let that sink in and took time to make eye contact with each of them. "If you want this, then hold nothing back. Now, let's take a moment of silence."

The room was silent. Rowe glanced around. Most of the Righters seemed deeply absorbed in thought. Jenna appeared to pray, while Princely seemed extremely anxious. All Rowe could hear was Maya's voice in her head. *You had better be praying child. Going up against the Jenroes is like facing the devil himself.* She chuckled to herself. She was beginning to feel that her mother might really be on to something with all of her sermons. She tried to shake the feeling, but something inside her confirmed that, in the end, they would need more than their own powers to be successful. It was beginning to sink in that without something bigger to believe in, completing this mission successfully would not be possible.

Why are these thoughts invading me now? Rowe thought, as she struggled to quiet the voice of her mother—Maya Pense entering her focus.

Suddenly, DiCaprio placed the story in her hand.

"It's all on you now," he said.

Rowe looked around the room at each Righter. Then she looked down at the papers and slowly opened them. A portal appeared before them. DiCaprio nodded, and they stepped through it.

∞∞∞∞∞∞∞∞∞∞

Once through the portal, they found themselves, yet again, in the laboratory of the compound. They knew they were in the story as each of them was suddenly heavily armed and in the combat gear that Rowe had penned.

"Connor implement Phase I of the Initiation," DiCaprio ordered.

Connor typed furiously on the computer. When he finished, he turned to everyone.

"Here we go guys. Phase I—Blackout."

Suddenly, they were surrounded by darkness.

"Righters, to your territories," DiCaprio ordered.

They each turned on their gear lights to see through the darkness. Jenna, Rowe, and Alfred were instructed to cover Righting while Xander, Princley, and DiCaprio left for Metisse.

DiCaprio continued, "Remember, inform the masses and

gather them. Provide them with arms if needed. Your most dangerous points are going to be the militia check points on ground and on the Rales. It's going to take the administration all night to figure out this black out, and when the lights come back on . . . we'll have a surprise for them!"

Connor was ordered to stay and man the computer system and begin Phase II of the Initiation at the crack of dawn, 0600. The Righters set out. Rowe could only imagine the complete pandemonium the darkness was causing in Imperium. They would have no idea what was going on. Signals connecting them to the other territories had been blocked. The holographic warning signs to the other territories were immediately visible in the dark skies. DiCaprio's voice rang out across the land.

To the people of the United Missions of America. Do you long to return to a life of liberty? Do you long to return to a life in which you are free in your pursuits of happiness, as in our history's days of old? We are citizens of the three oppressed territories. This is a coup. We are taking down the Jenroe administration. No more will we stand for inequality. No more will we stand for the killing of our children or the stealing of them from our homes! We will practice our faiths and preserve our culture on our own terms! Women heed our warning. Do not take the birth control. Our leaders are sterilizing you. They have declared genocide upon us! But no more will we be oppressed. Territories ban together. Organize! We are on our way to assist you. It is time to right a wrong that's been going on for over 1,000 years! We have now declared the Righting Wars!

∞∞∞∞∞∞∞∞∞

As the words rang out over and over, the people of Exilium began to cheer. Many took action immediately and overthrew the militia at all check points. Some of the militia even cheered and joined in with the citizens of the territories.

Each team arrived in its assigned territory on time at 0500. As Rowe, Alfred, and Jenna entered the Righting Territory, the citizens had already begun to overthrow the militia, which was largely outnumbered. The militia couldn't understand why the Jenroes were not sending the help they needed.

The sub-operatives that had been placed in the territories had organized many of the citizens, who were aware that the coup was about to begin. Alfred Pense stood in the middle of Main Street as citizens of Righting gathered around.

"We are here to help you," he announced. "Arm yourselves for protection only. Do not use these weapons unless completely necessary. We are the oppressed and we will not become the oppressor! We will take our liberty back the right way! We have one hour before the implementation of Phase II. Let's take our country back."

Alfred walked in the direction of the militia base where, for most of his life, he had reported to work every day. He now walked in as an enemy of the State, no longer the loyal and trusted brigadier general of Righting. He was the lead general in the Righting Wars.

∞∞∞∞∞∞∞∞∞∞

DiCaprio, Xander, and Princley came upon an identical scene in Metisse. The sub-operatives of Metisse had done their job of organizing the citizens, with only a few resisting. They anticipated some resistance in Metisse, but the only alternative the resisters had was to join forces with the militia, who were also outnumbered in Metisse, or fight on the side of the rebels. The Metisse were well aware that they would be slaughtered if they sought refuge in Imperium. Their resistance did not last very long. DiCaprio stood on the steps of Metisse Court as the citizens of Metisse gathered. The holographs appeared throughout the skies, and now his voice rang out among them as well. He gave a speech identical to the one Alfred Pense delivered in Righting.

"We have one hour," DiCaprio announced.

Chapter 22∞
KEELIE'S PERIL

Moments earlier, news media from all over Imperium swarmed the House of Missions' press room as Jackson Jenroe, the President's loyal brother, gave an emergency press conference on the Righting fugitives.

"Mr. Jenroe!" one reporter blurted out over a cacophony of others. "Exactly what is Alfred Pense and his family wanted for?"

"As we have previously stated, the Pense family has committed first-degree sedition, the most treasonous act against the laws of all the territories."

"Mr. Jenroe!" another reporter interjected, "are there any leads at this time on their whereabouts?"

"Not at this time. However, the administration is offering a reward for anyone who can lead us to their whereabouts and vows severe punishment for anyone who may be assisting them.

"Mr. Jenroe, sources say that Alfred Pense was in your custody but has subsequently escaped. Do you have any idea how he accomplished such a feat? Are not the militia prisons impossible from which to escape?"

Jackson faltered. He did not take kindly to the press asking questions that showcased the Jenroe administration's mistakes.

"That will be all for today," he said as he abruptly ended the press conference and stepped down from the podium.

∞∞∞∞∞∞∞∞∞∞

Keelie cautiously edged along the wall. She stopped just outside the Oval Office, an earshot away from the lodged door. She had to figure out what was going on. Jefferson was on to her. Somehow, he knew she had seen Rowe, and he made sure she was aware of it. But for some reason, he had left her to squirm. She strained to hear what was happening inside. Moments earlier, she had passed Jackson in the hallway. He had just left the press conference, and he didn't look pleased. She had waited for him to rejoin the president, Jefferson, and Madeline, then decided to eaves drop. But there were no conversations, only a strained silence in the room. She made out a few sounds of staffers nervously scuttling about.

She thought back over the past couple of days. Tensions had been high. Occasionally she overheard staffers mumbling, curious as to why the House of Missions was in such an uproar. She, too, wondered. This was not the first time that fugitives were at large for first-degree sedition, yet the administration had designated this as a territory-wide search.

She jolted at President Jenroe's booming voice.

"You may leave," he coldly announced. Keelie was certain he was addressing the staffers and militia she knew were in there.

"However, I want Imperium militia forces situated strategically in all territories, immediately!"

"That will not be possible," Jackson suddenly interrupted.

There was silence. Keelie imagined everyone in the room had turned to glare at him.

"What do you mean that will not be possible?" said President Jenroe.

Jackson cleared his throat. "Following the press conference, border security informed me that a force field of some kind has blocked entry into all territories, and have you not noticed that there is a blackout? National security is working on it all right now, but we are at a loss. It appears that all access points in and out of all the other territories, to and from Imperium, have been blocked as well."

"Jackson, you are such an imbecile," said the president. "Where is Patsy?"

Keelie cringed as it wasn't the first time the president had humiliated Jackson. He tended to get the brunt of the president's anger when there was chaos. Now he was using Patsy to insult Jackson's ability to lead.

"Did you hear me Jackson?" President Jenroe shouted.

"Where is Patsy?"

"We aren't sure. Travel logs show that she left during the early morning hours with a driver, but she failed to note her destination and hasn't returned."

"Has she not checked in?" the president asked.

"No, we have not heard from her."

Silence covered the room again.

"Why are you still standing there?" President Jenroe yelled as he slammed his fists onto his large wooden desk. Keelie presumed he was addressing the militia and staffers who had not fully exited. They must have been waiting for further orders following Jackson's unexpected announcement.

"Don't you have work to do? Get out of here! All of you! We have fugitives to catch! Get out!"

Keelie hurriedly slipped behind the angle of a wall in the hallway.

"What in the world is going on?" she heard one staffer nervously ask the other as they quickly exited the Oval Office.

"I'm not sure," the woman replied, but I am sure that this involves much more than first-degree sedition.

Keelie's heart pounded in her chest. *I have to get out of here.*

∞∞∞∞∞∞∞∞∞∞∞

Keelie raced to her living quarters. She quickly stuffed everything she could into her bag. Maybe Jefferson would not come looking for her before she had the chance to get out of there. She would go to her parent's home. The impulse to leave had hit her so impetuously she hadn't thought much about what she would do after that. Maybe she wouldn't have to do anything more but return to the safety of Jefferson's arms. Maybe her parents would have some good news, or maybe they could protect her. Although she still had not lost confidence in Jefferson, she no longer trusted the rest of the family—not even Madeline. And what of Patsy? Had Patsy been the one following her on the previous night? Keelie wasn't sure, but there was something innately sinister about her husband's aunt and she had never trusted her. Suddenly, the creak of the door startled her.

"Keelie, what are you doing? Are you going somewhere?"

It was Jefferson. Searching for words, she knew she had to appear as if her day was business-as-usual—if she had any hopes of getting away.

"Oh . . . oh . . . sweet heart, I'm just going to visit Mom and Dad."

"So, why are you taking clothes?"

"Oh . . . these things? I just thought I would grab something to lounge around in . . . you know . . . the patio can be really relaxing and beautiful this time of year."

Slowly and deliberately, Jefferson approached her. He relieved her of her bag. "Not today, Mrs. Jenroe. Not after last night."

"What?" Keelie asked with annoyance. "What about last night?"

"The accident," Jefferson replied. "I can tell by the way you are moving that you are still sore. Besides, the House of Missions has several garden areas for you to relax. I won't have you out and about again until you fully recuperate."

"But . . ."

"No buts. As a matter of fact, I would feel much better if you actually got a little bit of rest today." Slowly, from behind, Jefferson removed her sweater. His breath was hot on her neck.

"I want you to lie down, Keelie. It's good for you and the baby. Have you made an appointment with your new physician?"

Keelie paused. *How could Jefferson so casually ask about her new doctor and not even inquire about her friend, Dara? Was he so cold and angry at Dara that he had no concern for her safety? Or was he directly involved in her banishment to Exilium?*

"Umm . . . yes, I made an appointment," she said nervously. "She's a nurse practitioner and in charge of the practice until Dara's replacement is found. I've seen her before when Dara was on vacation. She's really good. I called her last night."

She struggled to avoid eye contact. He was acting suspiciously strange. She knew if she protested further, however, he would catch on. "I guess you're right. I'll get some rest."

"Good," Jefferson replied. "I'll see to it that we find you an appropriate physician. This Jenroe child will be delivered at the hands of a physician and a physician only."

"She has a doctorate," Keelie said, "and she's highly capable. I won't discuss this right now. It's my body and I have to be comfortable..."

"Okay . . . okay," said Jefferson, holding up his hands. "We will table this for now. Agreed?"

Keelie felt the heat in her cheeks. No Jenroe-appointed physician was going to deliver her child or take responsibility for the health of either of them. She didn't trust them. Out of the corner of her eye, she noticed Jefferson glaring at her. She succumbed to his wishes and slipped under the covers.

"Good girl," he whispered as he covered her with the blanket. "I'll be back to check on you within the hour."

She wasn't sure, but he seemed condescending.

Before he walked out of the room, he turned to face her.

"Don't worry, Keelie, this will be all over once the baby arrives."

Keelie's heart felt as if it were going to explode in her chest. There was something about the way he had spoken to her, the callous way he said it. For about ten minutes, she felt paralyzed. Then reality grasped her again.

"My cell!" she whispered to herself as she reached for it in a panic. She had missed three calls from her dad. Furiously, she dialed, hoping Jefferson wouldn't return.

"Dad? It's Keelie," she whispered.

"Hi Sweetie," Phil answered. "Are you okay? You sound scared."

"Dad, I need you to listen to me . . . I can't talk long."

"Okay, sweetie. I'm all ears."

"Dad . . . I think I'm in over my head . . ."

The bedroom door swung open. Madeline Jenroe stood in the opening. Keelie stared as she abruptly ended the call.

"Yes, dear, I completely agree," Madeline said. "You are way in over your head. Yes, you are."

Chapter 23∞
A CHANGE IN RIGHTING

The Jenroe stronghold on the militia base in Righting was expected to be a challenge. Sure enough, as soon as Jenna, Rowe, and Alfred set foot on the soil, unfriendly fire rang out. Instead of retreating, the citizens of Righting pushed forward. It was just enough to stun those of the coup, but not enough to prevent the brave mob from storming through the gates. Rowe's story, which included bullet-proof gear, had protected them all. No one was killed, only a few of the rebels were wounded.

Rowe found herself in immediate combat as she dropped to her knees to avoid the same round house kick her father had taught her to perfect. She went directly into a spin, sweeping three militia men off their feet and onto their backs.

Springing to her feet again, she noticed her father in hand-to-hand combat with two other men on the other side of the barrack entrance. A barrage of gunfire seemed to come from all directions. The choking smell of smoke invaded her lungs as she struggled to get to her father's side. A sense of panic overtook her as she could clearly see that more militia troops were headed his way with attack wolves. Jenna, who had the ability to control nature and animals, immediately kicked into gear. Before the wolves could close in on Alfred, she had complete control of them, and all of the attack animals were now fighting on the side of Righters. The militia began to retreat and surrender. White flags were being waved all over the Righting Territory.

∞∞∞∞∞∞∞∞∞∞

The Metisse Militia Base was larger than Righting and would be more difficult to take over. Fortunately, there were more people in Metisse, which provided a larger army for the Righters. The crowd stormed upon the militia base, as DiCaprio, Princley, and Xander led the way.

Xander released his surprise element, bolts of fire. The flaming weapons travelled throughout the grounds, catching the militia off guard. The ensuing confusion as they thought bombs were detonating caused this militia, too, to retreat. The three

Righters, along with the rebels of Metisse, stormed the militia building. As the attack wolves were released, DiCaprio immediately morphed into an alpha male and attacked the militia. All the other attack wolves turned on the militia and joined in assisting the rebels.

All of a sudden, an explosive amount of ammunition rained upon them from the top of the militia building. Princley Kerr took flight, landing a roundhouse kick upon the militia man operating the massive weapon, sending him plunging to the ground.

As the rosy glow of dawn began to illuminate the landscape, the militia of Metisse had yet to surrender. More and more militia men rained upon them. Xander and Princley made a quick decision. They hurriedly directed all the citizens of Metisse back to safety in the city.

"Retreat!" they yelled, "Retreat!"

The citizens withdrew. Just as the militia gained confidence that they had thwarted the rebellion, Princley took to the skies to see if they had made it to safety.

"Have the citizens taken refuge?" Xander yelled.

"Yes," Princley acknowledged from above.

DiCaprio ran for cover as the massive formation of militia men began to charge them. With all his energy, Xander generated a massive fire ball. He released it upon the charging militia, and the entire Metisse base exploded. Calmly, he and Jenna and DiCaprio walked away, as the Metisse militia base burned to the ground. It was now 0600 and the sun was above the horizon.

Connor Spaulding's voice rang through the skies of all the territories. "Implementing Phase II of the Initiation. Sunrise!" As the sun broke through the clouds in each of the territories, holographs began to disappear, yet, the words continued to ring clearly throughout. Signals sent messages to the electronic devices of all the homes. Televisions, radios, cell phones, bill boards, and all other devices displayed footage of the Righters successfully defeating the militia in their territories. Alfred, Jenna, and Rowe began the long walk back toward the underground passage in Exilium.

Suddenly, they were startled by the shrieking of tires. They jumped out of the way to avoid Keelie's car.

"What is she doing here?" Alfred barked.

Rowe sprinted toward her.

"Rowe, you can't!" Alfred warned.

The back window of the car rolled down.

"Rowe, I need to speak to you," said Keelie, who sat in the back seat donning dark sunglasses. Surprisingly, she seemed very calm.

"I'll be okay," Rowe called over her shoulder after talking to her. "She's taking me back to the compound."

Alfred felt uneasy. "Rowe, you're changing the story. You have to go back through the portal."

Before he could finish his words, Rowe was in the car and it sped off—and not in the direction of Exilium.

"Come on, Alfred, we have to get back," said Jenna. "Keelie would never hurt her. There must be an explanation."

Alfred knew something was terribly wrong. He was almost sure Rowe's story included Keelie being safe at the House of Missions.

∞∞∞∞∞∞∞∞∞∞

"Hey, where are we going?" Rowe yelled at the driver. "Keelie, what's going on?"

Suddenly, the smile that had greeted Rowe when she entered the car was gone. It was no longer Keelie who sat beside her.

"Hello, Rowe," said Patsy Hilleary. She swiftly administered an injection into Rowe's ribs. Pain exploded in Rowe's side. Suddenly all was dark.

Chapter 24∞
DOUBLE JEOPARDY

One by one, they all entered the underground passage to the compound. The portal was still there.

"Where's Rowe?" DiCaprio said, turning to Alfred with alarm.

"She was picked up by Keelie, who was returning her to Exilium."

"That wasn't a part of the plan," DiCaprio yelled. "This isn't good!" He paced back and forth. "Are you sure it was Keelie?"

"Yes, I'm sure!" said Alfred. "I saw her sitting in the back of the car, but honestly something seemed a little off, but Rowe never listens when it comes to that sister of hers."

"Why would Keelie be sitting in the back of her car?" DiCaprio questioned. "She would never get a driver to bring her here to see Rowe. It's too risky."

Beads of sweat began to break out on Alfred's forehead. "I'll go back and find Rowe. You guys go back through the portal."

Conner grabbed Alfred's arm. "No! It doesn't work like that, general. We all have to go back through the portal. Since Rowe's kidnapping wasn't written in, neither was a rescue. The good news is that they can't get out of Righting, wherever they've taken her, she's still in Righting. It's more dangerous to go back in the story. We have to go back in real time. We have to initiate another story."

Connor exited through the portal as the rest followed. As soon as everyone was back in the laboratory, the portal closed.

"Who's going to write, and what if it doesn't work?" Alfred asked, as the others murmured similar fears.

"My next best writer is Connor," said DiCaprio. He turned to him. "Can you do it?"

Connor appeared apprehensive. "I'm not as good as Rowe."

"You can do it!" DiCaprio said. "You have to. You're the only hope she has."

Connor immediately sat down and began writing. The others stood by and waited in nervous silence. After a few minutes, he sat the pen down, and a portal opened.

"Here," he said, handing the story over to DiCaprio. "Look over it quickly. Something tells me we don't have enough time. I have a feeling that wasn't Keelie who picked up Rowe. It could have very well been Patsy Hilleary."

"No," said Alfred Pense. "I'm sure it was Keelie."

Connor was visibly unsettled.

DiCaprio frowned. "Is there something you're not telling us, Connor?"

Connor grabbed his jacket, and appeared agitated. "Just trust me on this one. Patsy Hilleary has the ability to morph. She could have easily morphed into Keelie. The good news, DiCaprio, is they do not know you. Have you finished reviewing the story?"

"Yes," said DiCaprio, glancing again suspiciously at Connor.

"Let's go," Connor said, as he entered the portal. DiCaprio followed, but not before looking back at the other Righters.

When they reached the other side of the portal, they found

themselves on Main Street of Righting.

"They have the girl," an old vagabond eerily warned.

"Where did they take her?" DiCaprio demanded.

The man did not answer, but he pointed in the direction of Righting Court.

∞∞∞∞∞∞∞∞∞∞

"Keelie? Rowe mumbled as she gained consciousness. The pain from the injection exploded in her ribs once again.

I don't think Keelie can hear you," an evil voice answered. "She's safely tucked away in Imperium, and you, my dear, are in Righting. Are you aware of the punishment for treason?"

Rowe struggled to see. The thick blackness of the room and the haziness from the injection clouded her sight. She could only make out a shadow of the evil woman who had abducted her. Though it was dark, she could almost feel the woman's cold glare boring into her. Rowe tried to focus. Maybe a few men from the militias made it into hiding and assisted whoever this was in taking her to this dark basement in Righting Court.

"What did you do with Keelie?" Rowe managed to say, as she rolled over in pain on the floor of the cold room.

"We are not here to discuss Keelie, Miss Sparrow. We are

here because you have committed treason against the United Missions of America. How do you plead?"

Rowe did not answer.

"Shock her!" Patsy demanded.

Suddenly a piercing bolt of electricity and a furious heat overtook Rowe's entire body. She yelled out in excruciating pain. Suddenly, darkness settled upon her once again.

∞∞∞∞∞∞∞∞∞∞

"Stop, Patsy!"

Patsy Hilleary pivoted toward the voice. Through the pitch black, she saw that it was President Jeremy Jenroe. He flipped on the lights and she was suddenly blinded.

"Give me my glasses," she demanded to the militia. She quickly donned the dark glasses. They were not as effective as complete darkness, but she could now see Jeremy standing before her.

"How did you get here?" she demanded. "The Rebels have blocked off all access to Imperium."

"I have my ways, Patsy," Jenroe replied. "You've done well. I've come to retrieve the girl."

"Get her!" Jenroe ordered the militia man at his side who

picked Rowe up in his arms.

Patsy squinted and tilted her head to adjust her sight under the dark glasses. There was something awfully familiar about the militia man accompanying Jenroe.

"Where are you taking her?" Patsy asked.

"Back to Imperium," Jenroe responded. "We have big plans for little Miss Sparrow."

"How am I to get back to Imperium?" Patsy demanded.

"The access that I have acquired is only for me, Patsy. We are working on it. You may re-enter Imperium within a couple of days. Stay here until I send further word."

Patsy stared after them. The basement door clicked shut.

∞∞∞∞∞∞∞∞∞∞

Rowe slowly began to rouse. The sky above her was blurry. She thought she was moving but wasn't sure. She tried to keep her eyes open, but she was still too groggy from the shock that had sent her back into darkness. Where am I? she thought. She began to recognize the voice of President Jenroe directing the militia man who carried her.

As they quickly turned the corner onto Main Street, Rowe knew she needed to fight for her life. President Jenroe would kill her. Unable to feel much of her body, she swung her fist as best she could with a right hook. It sent the helmet of the militia man flying into the streets. Immediately, she recognized Connor.

"Connor?" she questioned through her haze.

"Yes," replied the president, who suddenly morphed back into DiCaprio. "That is Connor." The fear in Rowe gave way to tears. She was exhausted and tired.

When they arrived at the portal on Main Street, they immediately stepped back through. Once again, they found themselves in the laboratory of the compound. Conner set Rowe down on her feet. She held onto his arm to steady herself and looked around the room. All of the Righters, along with her mom and dad, were looking at her. Her dad's eyes were moist with tears.

"What's going on?" asked Rowe, as she struggled to regain coherency. "What happened?"

DiCaprio smiled. "I'll tell you what's happened, Miss Sparrow. We did it. We successfully implemented The Righting Wars—the Initiation is complete.

Chapter 25∞
Fresh Flowers

Philmore Sparrow wasn't his usual self. Always the one attempting to maintain the cheer in the home, he was now overly anxious. There was still no word from Keelie. He had not heard from her since their call was terminated abruptly. He had repeatedly tried to call her back. Each time, it went directly to voice mail.

"Jana . . . Jana!" Philmore shouted, fully aware she was inebriated on the back patio by the pool trying, once again, to drown out her worries.

"What is it, Phil?" she slurred, as she took another gulp from the wine glass.

Philmore couldn't believe she was once again drowning in alcohol. Honestly, he actually could believe it. She had never stopped, and he had had enough. He walked through the patio door and slammed it shut, furious.

"Do you even try?" he shouted as he stood over her intoxicated body. He noticed that she didn't even flinch. He knew she could hear the fury in his voice, but she sat there, ignoring him, frozen in her own drunken world.

"If you can free yourself from the wine bottle for a moment, you may be interested to know that Keelie called, and she is terrified," he continued.

Jana sighed and slowly turned to face him. What Philmore saw broke his heart. Her beautiful blue eyes were bloodshot and swollen. He could tell that she had been crying for hours.

"I know why!" she said. "They are dead, Philmore. I already know it!"

Philmore frowned. "Dead? What are you talking ab...?"

"Dead!" Jana sobbed, "I already know . . ."

"Jana, calm down. Keelie did not say anything . . ."

"Philmore!" Jana yelled, "It never pays to keep secrets. There are no fresh flowers on the grave."

∞∞∞∞∞∞∞∞∞∞

Keelie sat on the bed, speechless; staring at Madeline's foreboding presence in the doorway. She had always trusted her, but now she didn't know who was safe to trust.

"I'm sorry, Madeline," she stuttered. "I was speaking..."

"I know who you were speaking with," Madeline softly replied. "Come . . . come with me, dear. We can talk privately in the rose garden."

Keelie carefully swung her legs over the side of the bed and stood up, without taking her eyes off of Madeline. "Let me grab my sweater, and I'll meet you out there."

"Oh, I'll wait," Madeline responded. "Jefferson tells me that you've been a little under the weather. We wouldn't want anything to happen to our little Jenroe, now would we?"

Keelie only half smiled. She couldn't decipher if Madeline was showing genuine concern or being cynical, but she knew she had to play along.

As they walked down the halls of the House of Missions, Keelie noticed there was no staff. No longer were they scurrying about aimlessly as if the entire building were burning down. However, she heard President Jenroe belligerently spewing orders to his minions.

"Oh, never mind him," Madeline chuckled.

Keelie cleared her throat. "I'm used to it."

Madeline smiled. "Yes, I guess so. How could you not be?"

The rose garden was as beautiful as ever under a bright spring sky. The scent of the blossoms seemed to be Keelie's only ally at the moment. They always had a calming effect.

"Have a seat dear," Madeline gestured, as they approached the wrought iron benches located in the midst of the largest blooms. Keelie obliged her, not really knowing what to say. At that point, she felt silence was her best option.

"Oh, Keelie, Keelie. Dear, sweet Keelie," Madeline verbosely sang as she softly caressed Keelie's cheek. "What were you thinking, dear, when you joined this family?"

"Wh . . . what?" Keelie asked, as if confused. She slightly turned away, pulling back from Madeline.

Silently, Madeline turned to face her directly. "Oh, dear, it's just us now. No surveillance, no Jenroe men. You can let your guard down now."

"I'm not sure what you mean."

"Well, I will tell you what I mean," Madeline replied.

317

"You don't have to say a word. Just listen. Deal?"

"Sure . . . I mean . . . I'll listen," Keelie stuttered.

Her mother-in-law chuckled. "Dear . . . you married into the Jenroes—the most ruthless leaders in the history of this country. In the history of the world, some would argue."

Madeline's laughter troubled Keelie. She couldn't get a good read on her but continued to listen.

"The tragedy in all of this," Madeline continued, "is that I don't doubt for one minute that you love my son, and I can assure you that he loves you as well. However, your uncle Jackson loved his wife, Aniston, too."

Madeline paused and glared at Keelie with a raised brow. Keelie suddenly sensed that her mother-in-law was warning her.

"Unfortunately, it was Aniston's love for humanitarian rights that made her dispensable," said Madeline.

Keelie felt she said it a little too aloofly. She turned to stare at her. How could she be so indifferent when speaking of Aniston? For God's sake, the woman's dead.

"I was very fond of Aniston," said Madeline. "She was a very beautiful woman. You remind me of her quite a bit. The blond hair and the striking blue eyes. Yes, that was Aniston—so beautiful—inside and out. Honestly, I think you remind Jeremy of her too." Madeline's face suddenly went flat.

Keelie crossed her arms tightly around herself. The thought of her reminding Jeremy of a deceased woman made her skin crawl.

"Oh, it's not the hair or the eyes, however. It's your bleeding heart dear," Madeline firmly spoke. "Oh, Keelie . . . you sweet, unassuming creature. I have survived Jeremy by hiding my heart. I am still here because he's never known that side of me. I had a conversation very similar to this with that lovely sister-in-law of mine over a decade ago. She was such a delicate and darling woman. I really liked her, you know, and I am sure that if she were here, she would subtly inform you that when you are with Jenroe child, and you cross Jeremy Jenroe, not only do you become no more than an incubator to this family, but, darling, you surely mark yourself as dispensable. Oh, how I wish Aniston were here to share this with you." Madeline sighed. ". . . but, she's not. Unfortunately for her, Keelie, Jeremy despised her heart."

Suddenly, Madeline's tone became serious. Keelie watched the look on her face become grave, and her own began to flood with tears. She could feel her heart pounding through the walls of her chest and her breathing quickened. She focused on the calming scent of the English roses in the garden. If it were not for them, she knew she would enter into a full-blown panic attack.

"Listen carefully to me, Keelie," Madeline coldly spoke. "Your father-in-law despises anyone who has a bleeding heart— because he has no heart. And he has an unexplainable power over Jackson, and even Jefferson. Once the baby is no longer inside of you, he will not hesitate to literally and physically rip . . . your . . . heart . . .out."

Chapter 26∞
INITIATION COMPLETE

When Rowe awoke, she had no idea how long she had been out. DiCaprio had deactivated the voice recognition as to give Dara access to the room, and the Righters took shifts sitting in, but Alfred and Maya had spent the last 24 hours at their daughter's bedside. In her deepest sleep, Rowe could hear Maya praying at her bedside, and for once, it didn't seem as annoying as it had in the past. She was just comforted to hear her mother's voice.

"Mom, is that you?" she asked, as she groaned and stretched.

"I'm right at your side, Rowe," Maya softly spoke.

"Mom, we did it." Rowe whispered through her

discomfort and exhaustion.

"I know," Maya chuckled. "Your father told me, but I never doubted you . . . I prayed—a lot . . . but never doubted you."

Rowe attempted to lift herself in the bed, but she was still weak from the injection and the electric shock, with very sore ribs to prove it.

"Don't try to get up, sweetie," said Maya. "Dara says you need your rest."

Through blurred vision, Rowe could see the outline of her mother's face. Suddenly, her mind went back to the day her parents went missing, the day it had all begun . . . the empty house . . . the thought of losing her parents . . . and the letters.

For a moment, she thought her parents had left her side, but the soft scent of Maya's perfume told Rowe that her mother was still near. She was glad, because she had to ask about the letters. So much had happened that she had forgotten about them, and she wanted to ask, but the need for sleep was winning a battle that she could no longer fight.

"Mom," she weakly called out.

"Yes, dear?"

Rowe succumbed to letting some seconds pass—she wasn't sure how many— but they had slipped by in silence as she continued to fight against the sleep caused by the pain medications that Dara had given her. Before she let herself completely drift off to sleep again, she rustled herself awake.

"Mom?" she whispered.

"Yes, dear?"

"Who is Pammy? And who is YSTP?"

She could fight sleep no more, but before she closed her eyes, she glimpsed the unsettled looks in the eyes of both of her parents.

∞∞∞∞∞∞∞∞∞∞

Rowe's vision slowly came into focus. She could see an image sitting there, watching over her. At first, she was sure it was DiCaprio.

"How long have I been out?" she asked.

"Two days," the voice replied.

She immediately recognized Connor's voice.

"Whoa . . . hold on there, Rowe," he said as she collapsed, trying to pull herself up in bed. "Here, I'll help you."

As Connor gently pulled her up in the bed, and fluffed the

pillow behind her, he clearly came into focus. His eyes were amazing, and in her sleepy stupor she said it aloud.

"Your eyes are amazing."

"Yeah, I already heard you," Connor said aloofly, chuckling.

Rowe quickly turned away, embarrassed. For a moment, she had forgotten that Connor could read her thoughts.

"Just don't look directly at me," he said. "And if you concentrate hard enough, you can block me out . . . I told you before . . . you're a tough one, Rowe."

"Where is everyone?" she asked.

"Oh, they are dispersed around the compound. Some are out in Exilium, training and organizing. We were able to secure the routes connecting Exilium and Metisse, and no one from Imperium can get in. We did it, Rowe."

"Yeah, and I almost destroyed all our hard work," Rowe replied with a sigh of exhaustion.

"How did you and DiCaprio find me?"

"I was manning all the entries into the territories. I knew one of the Jenroe vehicles had entered, but it was too late. At first it appeared it was just a driver. When Alfred and Jenna told me it was Keelie, I knew it couldn't be because the territory monitor told me Keelie had made it back to Imperium safely."

"So that means you had an idea that someone was impersonating Keelie?" Rowe suspiciously probed. "But what would give you that idea?"

Connor was silent. He began to pace the room. Then turned to her and sighed.

"Connor Spalding is not my true identity. Six years ago, at the age of sixteen, I faked my own death. My real name is Jackson Jenroe, Jr."

Rowe gasped in horror. She began to push herself away from Connor. He put his hand gently on her arm.

"Just hear me out, Rowe. I promise I won't harm you."

"I was born a Righter. My family was well aware of it, but because I was a Paler, they decided to keep me and keep it hidden from the rest of the administration. The location of my mark is fairly obvious."

Connor lifted his shirt to show the mark in the center of his back.

"My uncle Jeremy was not happy about it at all, and he was always very cruel to me. For a long time, my mother and I stayed at the House of Missions with my uncle and aunt because my father traveled all the time throughout the territories. Right after I turned 15, my mother went missing. I was told by my father that she abandoned me and relocated somewhere in Europe, and that was all I knew, at least for a while. Needless to say, I was left in the care of Uncle Jeremy and Aunt Maddie.

Aunt Maddie was a kind woman and a very good person. Unfortunately, a couple of months after my mother's disappearance, I overheard my father Jackson Sr. and Uncle Jeremy talking about my mother. I heard my father admit to killing her himself. He laughed about how she had begged for her life, and how he killed her because she had empathy for the other territories... just like Keelie.

I remembered my mother talking about Visera all the time, so I sought her out. I disguised myself as a Metisse and made my way to Exilium. Visera helped me to fake my own death and memory loss. She confirmed for the orphanage that I was truly an orphan and that my name was Connor Spalding."

"Keelie told me about you," said Rowe. "I mean, she talked about how you died in a plane crash headed to Exilium."

"Yes, that's me. I'm the dead cousin of the powerful

Jenroe family. When my mother went missing, my instinct was to suspect Jeremy Jenroe of killing her, but knowing the truth made it even worse. Uncle Jeremy always pitted Jefferson and me against one another. Jefferson always viewed me as a real threat to his political ambitions because of the mark, but I wanted nothing to do with the politics of that family. I met your biological family when Keelie was dating Jefferson. So, of course, I know Keelie. I didn't want to get close to you because I didn't want to take the chance of any of your family discovering me.

"I lived most of my life in the Jenroe household, and they are the cruelest and most vile people I have ever known Rowe. My Aunt Patsy is maniacal. She is blind but can see in darkness, and she can morph into other people. I knew it was her and not Keelie on the day of the Initiation when you were kidnapped. I was sure of it. I, as much as you, want to destroy the Jenroes. They killed my mother, Rowe. They killed her.

Keelie . . . she's just like my mother, the complete opposite of those people. Aunt Maddie is somewhat neutral. She doesn't have a bleeding heart for the Sunzes and Metisses, but she doesn't spew hate for them either.

When DiCaprio and I rescued you, I was prepared to

reveal myself to Patsy, if that meant saving you. That is how I knew, Rowe. That is how I knew."

A thick silence covered the room. Rowe slowly sat up and put her arms around Connor, who was sobbing. "We won't let them get away with this, Connor," she softly whispered. "This is only the beginning. We have something they don't have, Connor."

Rowe sat back and reached over to open the drawer to her bedside table. From there, she retrieved a small stack of papers and presented them to Connor. "Yes, the Initiation was a success. But we have much more. We have the next Righting Wars, the Infiltration—and we will fight them until the end."

The End

ABOUT THE AUTHOR

    M.J. Logan is an avid reader and writer of speculative fiction, with Christian fantasy being her favorite genre. She strongly believes that those of us who wish to use our gifts from God to change the world are "RIGHTERS". With three Amazon Best Sellers under her belt from her debut fantasy books-- The Maurpikios Fiddler series, she now introduces the world to her new Trilogy- The Righting Wars with Book 1-- *The Initiation* as the first release. It is her hope that through her writing she will continue to promote unity and hope throughout the world for those with a love for fantasy fiction and all genres. She resides in the Southeastern United States with her husband and two sons, and her favorite charity is St. Jude's Children's Research Hospital in Memphis, Tennessee.

EPIOLOGUE

"WRITERS" ARE "RIGHTERS"

I was born during a time in my country where there was more opportunity for me than those like me, that had come before me. I attended a school that had a diverse population of people. If ever I had experienced a negative encounter as a child, I was more than likely too naïve to know any better. For that, I am happy and surely feel blessed. However, my experiences as a child surely preserved my innocence and my belief that nothing was impossible for any of us to accomplish. While I understood that there was both good and bad in this world, I still believed with all my heart that there was always a way to find good in everyone and every situation.

I dreamed of being a RIGHTER as a child. As a little girl I would pretend I had super powers from God that would help me to change the world—to right wrongs. Of course, as we all do, I grew up one day and realized that saving and changing the world was not and still is not an easy feat. I knew even as a child that a RIGHTER is not just someone who does something because they feel passionate about it, RIGHTERs Choose to do what's right. However, I will tell you that I no longer wish to be a RIGHTER… I know that I already am… We all have the Gifts of the

"RIGHTER".

I had not thought about the term "RIGHTER" for years. The concept came back to me in a dream during the most recent election in our country. I saw the unity, the beautiful concept that my country represented being destroyed each day by hate, judgement, bias, cruelty and all the little "isms" that began to creep their way into the mainstream of our society.

People were failing to communicate with one another, and many people were painting each other with one large brush stroke. I wanted to make things right, but I didn't know what to do or how to do it. Then one day it hit me! I realized that I learned many lessons in life over the years, and one of those lessons I learned is that children are not born with hate in their hearts. Children are not born with bias, and children are not born being judgmental. Unfortunately, the world exposes children to these things, and those of us who are adults must find ways to counter the negativity, the loss of love, and the threat to our unity as a diverse world, but sometimes we must be reminded of it.

I know that it is hard to believe that we are all "RIGHTERS", but we are not a "RIGHTER" in the sense that the characters in this book are. We are RIGHTERS, in the sense that God has given all of us the gift of RIGHTERS, we just have to be willing to use them.

We don't have the ability to read the minds of others, but we do have the ability to listen and try to see things from their perspective. We don't have the ability to control the thoughts of others, but we do have the ability to help someone to feel better or smile. We don't have the ability to literally fly, but we can soar and reach for the stars in all that we do and encourage others to do so as well. We do not have the ability to communicate with nature, but we can love and appreciate, and take care of this beautiful world that God has given us. We do not have the ability to literally start fires, but we can start a revolution of innovation and spiritual awakening unlike ever seen!

However, there is one special Gift of the RIGHTER that many of us do have, and that is the ability to Write Stories. Yes, like Rowe we can write stories that can change the world! Stories that can change history as we know it, and stories that can "Right" all that is wrong. I realized as I have witnessed people refuse to listen to the perspective of others or refuse to put themselves in someone else's shoes that there was a true lack of empathy among us, so I decided to use my gift as a RIGHTER... and Write a story. I found it quite disturbing that people were no longer listening to one another, so the child in me hoped that if people refuse to listen to one another, then maybe... just maybe, they we will listen to the characters in my story.

Maybe they will see in this story the true turmoil that people experience when they want to make a difference, but don't know how or even where to begin. Maybe they will see the hurt that someone experiences when they are judged by what they look like, where they were born, or what religious group they belong to, and not by what is in their hearts.

If in life you ever encounter a person who says something or does something that is hurtful or angers you, just remember as "RIGHTERS" we must always do what's right and consider that maybe... just maybe... at some point in their lives that person was wronged and did not have a "RIGHTER" to come their rescue.

So, guys, I invite you to follow me in this trilogy as I attempt to bring about understanding, empathy, love and peace throughout our beautiful world. However, I want each of you to remember that not everyone is bad, and just because someone does not agree with you on one thing, does not mean that you don't have many other things in common. We have to come together and have empathy for one another if we wish to preserve this beautiful concept of America and a global society. Remember…

"If a house be divided against itself, that house cannot stand. Mark3:25) KJV.

    I hope you enjoy! Stay tuned for book II of the Righting Wars- The Infiltration!

Be blessed,

M. J. Logan

M.J. Logan

A Sneak Peek at other books AND WHERE TO FIND M.J. Logan

MAURPIKIOS FIDDLER: THE TRUE MEANING OF MAGIC~ Book 1- Faith

Amazon Best Seller and Reader's Favorite- 5 Star

In the small town of Hallows Creek beware of what you assume; things are not always what they seem. The Fiddler's appearing to be the picture-perfect family, but they harbor deep dark secrets that are about to be unleashed on the stability of an entire world. Even after realizing the terrible twin diseases are one in the same, childhood cancer and scorpioma, it is still a race to save the lives of their children. A century old treaty had ended years of war and is now vulnerable to a long-held prophecy that foretells the emergence of a champion. Could that Champion be young Maurpikios Fiddler? Unfortunately, for every champion, there will be dark forces to oppose his greatness. Radu Vrotsos, a wealthy philanthropist and a maniacal wizard, is vehemently against the integration of the magicals and the non-magicals. It is his hope to bring the world to submission under one of the darkest and evil powers in existence.

A sudden attack of excruciating headaches and horrifying dreams will be the horrific antecedent to Maurpikios Fiddler's journey. Unexpectedly, he will find himself in the position of facing down the enemy as well as his own mortality. He swiftly soars into a world of chaos where he is suddenly exposed to the staunch reality of magic intertwined with danger, curses, evil witches and wizards and infinite adventure. This magically enchanting quest involves other children like himself, a scroll that reveals the secrets of a family, a golden scepter and a stone destined only for the hands of the chosen one. Maurpikios Fiddler will discover just how the secrets of the Fiddler family affect his own destiny and the entire town of Hallows Creek. He will have no choice but to display true bravery, accept his destiny, and ultimately discover the True Meaning of Magic.

ꟿAURPIKIOS ꟿIDDLER: ꟘHE ꟿAGICAL AMETHYST OF ꟅPES~
Book 2- Hope
Amazon Best Seller and Reader's Favorite- 5 Star

Secrets of the town of Hallows Creek continue to unfold as the children and the medical staff of Saint Juliana's continue fighting for the stability of the research study and the Treaty of Earthly Peace. Maurpikios Fiddler and the others have returned to school to begin their seventh-grade year, but the chosen one- young Maurpikios Fiddler has a secret that he has yet to reveal. Saint Juliana has told him that he must be the one to find the six remaining Legacy Stones.

The forces of good and evil are imbalanced and are having

a great impact on the entities of health and sickness throughout the land, especially in the town of Hallows Creek. Once again, the race is on, but this time to find the Amethyst of Spes, and to restore the magic that was discovered at Saint Juliana's. Many are still depending on the on the old ways of the magical world and have forgotten *The True Meaning of Magic.* Maurpikios Fiddlers and the others along with the warriors of Saint Juliana's are once again determined to restore hope and balance to the world, and most of all to teach everyone how to remember the magic.

Maurpikios Fiddler: The Red Ruby of Edo~ **Book 3- Love**
Amazon Best Seller and Reader's Favorite- 5 Star

The world's fate united by the Treaty of Earthly Peace lies in the hands of Piki and the children of the prophecy. They are catapulted into a chaotic race to awaken the only being with the power to reverse the calamitous spell of perpetual seasons. The Amulet of Salvere maintained faith. The Amethyst restored hope, and now The Red Ruby of Edo has a heart to heal, but nothing has prepared them for the wrath of Nivalis!

Fans!

Stay tuned for the remaining four books in the Maurpikios

Fiddler Series!!!!!

And...

The Righting Wars II- The Infiltration

Coming In 2019!

All M.J Logan Titles Available on www.mjlogan.net

Amazon.com, Barnes and Nobles, and other Online

Retailers!

You can follow M.J. on

www.mjlogan.net

www.Mjloganbooks.com

https://Facebook.com/Mjlogan8149

https://twitter.com/Mjlogan8149

https://www.goodreads.com/mjlogan8149

And Always Remember...

THERE IS MAGIC IN THE AIR!

M.J. LOGAN